Blake didn't know whether he wanted to kill her or kiss her.

"Sydney, do you remember my telling you that I came to Ocean City to *work?*" he asked in frustration.

Sydney shook her head. "Nope. But now that you mention it, you've been sitting at your desk all morning staring out the window. You might want to move the desk. Mom always makes sure her desk faces a blank wall or else, she says, she'll be distracted."

Sydney's words made up his mind. He wanted to kill her. All that dancing and prancing, and those skimpy outfits—how much of it had been for his benefit? Blake narrowed his eyes. "You *knew* I could see you?"

Her grin widened. "Every minute," she admitted, her emerald eyes large and innocent.

Blake looked down into her smiling face. "You ought to come with a warning label, Sydney!"

Dear Reader,

The festive season is often so hectic—a whirlwind of social calls, last-minute shopping, wrapping, baking, tree decorating and finding that perfect hiding place for the children's gifts! But it's also a time to pause and reflect on the true meaning of the holiday: love, peace and goodwill.

Silhouette Romance novels strive to bring the message of love all year round. Not just the special love between a man and woman, but the love for children, family and the community, in stories that capture the laughter, the tears and, *always,* the happy-ever-afters of romance.

I hope you enjoy this month's wonderful love stories—including our WRITTEN IN THE STARS selection, *Arc of the Arrow* by Rita Rainville. And in months to come, watch for Silhouette Romance titles by your all-time favorites, including Diana Palmer, Brittany Young and Annette Broadrick.

The authors and editors of Silhouette Romance books wish you and your loved ones the very best of the holiday season . . . and don't forget to hang the mistletoe!

Sincerely,

Valerie Susan Hayward
Senior Editor

KASEY MICHAELS

Sydney's Folly

Published by Silhouette Books New York

America's Publisher of Contemporary Romance

To my brother, Don Charles, and his wife, Marie,
and to my sister, Bonnie Charles Brosious, and her
husband, Carl. It took three tries, but this time, by
golly, we made it! I love you, guys!

SILHOUETTE BOOKS
300 E. 42nd St., New York, N.Y. 10017

SYDNEY'S FOLLY

ISBN: 0-373-08834-5

First Silhouette Books printing December 1991

Printed in the U.S.A.

KASEY MICHAELS,

the author of more than two dozen books, divides her creative time between Silhouette Romance and Regency romance novels. Married and the mother of four, Kasey's writing has garnered the Romance Writers of America Golden Medallion Award and the *Romantic Times* Best Regency Trophy.

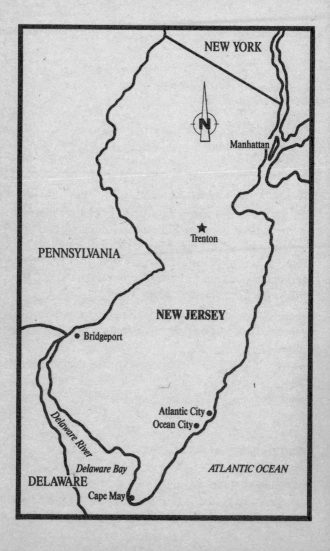

Chapter One

Sydney Blackmun slowly counted to three, then held her breath and carefully lifted her hands from the life-size ceramic figure.

"It worked! Do you see that, oh ye of the snide remarks and precious little faith in your immensely modest big sister's talents? I told you this would be a great educational experience. Determination, perseverance—and the judicious application of some handy dandy miracle glue—and Herbert is back, as good as new! So now what do you guys have to say for yourselves?"

"An *educational* experience?" Paul Richardson, who had been sprawled on the wooden front porch beside his sister, watching as Sydney reattached one ear to the ceramic dalmatian she had rescued from a garage sale, pulled a face and added, "I guess you could call it that. We did learn something all right,

Syd. We learned that good old Herb is still ugly now that he's got two ears. *Big* and ugly.''

"Big and ugly and still *one*-eared,'' his twin Pete corrected from his vantage point near the porch steps, pointing toward the dalmatian—and the ear that was slowly slipping down the side of its long throat. "Great hang time on that string of glue, though, sis, I'll give you that. Paul and I think maybe you'd better give up on this one. Isn't that right, bro? It really hurts us to see our sister fail.''

"Yeah. It isn't a pretty sight.''

"Never!'' Sydney grabbed at the ear just before the glue failed completely, then stuck it back where it belonged. "Sydney Blackmun doesn't know the meaning of the word defeat! I just didn't hold the stupid ear in place long enough or something, that's all.''

As if acting on some silent signal known only to themselves, Paul and Pete rose at the same time and headed for the full flight of broad wooden steps that led down to the street, two identical black-haired boys of eleven, whose thin, gangly legs seemed to have sprouted like fast-growing weeds from the hems of their matching neon yellow-and-purple swim trunks.

"Yeah, right,'' Pete agreed with his sister, commiseratingly. "You just *stick* in there all afternoon and keep working on that ear, Syd. Sounds like a great way to spend the day. But now that the tide's coming in we're heading up to the Eighth Street beach to watch those college guys on their surfboards. They sure know how to put on the moves.''

"Yeah,'' Paul added, tripping down the steps behind him. "They're really something else! I want to go to college in California, where the really big waves are, so I can learn how to move that way.''

''As long as all your 'moves' remain confined to surfboards, buddy boy,'' Sydney answered absently, adding, ''and don't go stuffing your faces with pizza while you're on the boardwalk. I've got a meat loaf mixed and ready to go in the microwave.''

The twins exchanged painfully amused grimaces as they echoed together, ''Nuclear meat loaf. Oh, yummy.''

Sydney wasn't insulted. She had set herself two projects this summer. Restoring this old house, and learning how to cook a decent meal. The house could certainly be said to be coming along, if somewhat slowly, with only a few detours, like Herbert, along the way. But so far she wasn't giving Julia Child anything to worry about.

''Don't panic, guys. I left out the eggs this time. How was I to know you're supposed to take the shells off first? They looked so cute in that magazine picture—two entire cooked eggs snuggled inside the loaf.''

''Well, next time you'd better read the directions, 'cause they didn't look so *cute* splattered all over the kitchen,'' Pete teased, nudging his brother in the ribs before taking off down the sidewalk at a fast trot, his bare feet slapping against the cement.

Paul turned to follow, nearly cannoning into a tall, slim man carrying a large cardboard box toward the house next door. ''Whoops! Sorry about that, sir,'' he mumbled sheepishly, putting out his hands to help steady the box.

The man smiled down at him. "Don't worry about it. No harm, no foul," the man said, continuing on his way toward the flight of steps attached to the side of the two-story house.

"Thank you, sir," Paul replied quickly, looking past the man to see that his brother had nearly reached the ramp leading up to the boardwalk. "Yo, sis!" he called in a carrying voice, already rapidly backpedaling toward the boardwalk, "Do ya think we can all go up to Tenth Street for frozen yogurt after dinner? Unless you're still holding on to that ear."

Sydney gingerly removed her hand from the ceramic ear and watched as the piece immediately dropped to the porch floor.

"Sure," she answered automatically, beginning a search for the tube of glue—the one whose label had boasted of the ability of its contents to instantly and permanently bond to any surface.

"Oh, that's great! That's just *great!*" she exploded a few seconds later, finding the open tube with her left knee.

She stood, and the tube stood with her, firmly stuck to her skin. "I wonder what *Consumer Reports* magazine would have to say about this stuff," she grumbled, about to grab at the tube. "Don't do that, Sydney," she admonished herself quickly, jerking her fingers away, "or else you'll end up with a hand stuck to your knee. And wouldn't *that* be a pretty picture!"

Left with no other options, and with the twins gone, Sydney began an impromptu hop-hop around the porch in an effort to shake the tube loose.

"What in the hell—?" Blake Mansfield stopped in his tracks, staring up at the girl who seemed to be doing a war dance around a large ceramic dalmatian, while occasionally hopping perilously close to the edge of the curved wooden porch that had been stripped of its protective railing.

She was going to fall off the side any moment now and kill herself, he decided. Just as quickly he realized that such an event would be a terrible waste, for— even as she lurched around awkwardly, seemingly intent on shaking her left knee free of her body—she was quite the loveliest woman he had seen in a while. A long while.

Her hair was as long and straight and black as midnight. Her tall, sleek body, clothed in cutoff faded denims and a skimpy hot pink tank top, radiated health and beauty in equal measure. Her skin, tanned to a soft honeyed darkness, made him think of sand and surf and long walks on a moonlit beach.

"You'll be waxing poetic in a minute, Mansfield," he muttered aloud. Blake shook his head, bringing himself back to reality as he deposited the cardboard box on the first step of the stairway. He trotted across the narrow cement driveway and onto the sparse, sandy lawn that surrounded the house next door to his rented condo, prepared to catch her if she fell.

But she had stopped hopping and was now seated on the edge of the porch, her bare legs dangling above the ground as she watched him approach.

"Hi, there," she greeted him breezily. The sight of her whiter-than-white smile, which told him without words that she knew he had witnessed her dance—and

hoped it had amused him—delivered a powerful, figurative and not totally unexpected roundhouse to
Blake's midsection. "Lovely day, isn't it? Not a cloud
in sight."

Oh yes, she was a beauty all right. Beautiful and
friendly and very intriguing. If he had a single functioning brain cell in his head, he'd turn on his heels
and run for the hills.

"And hello to you," he replied with studied ease,
stopping directly in front of her, so that her bare toes
nearly grazed his right shoulder. "I didn't mean to
trespass, but for a moment there I was afraid you were
going to do a swan dive off the porch."

Sydney looked down at the man and saw that he was
almost but not quite openly laughing at her. End-
lessly fascinated with her fellow man, she had known
at a glance that he must be Mrs. Harwick's upstairs
tenant, and she had been pleased to see that he was
fairly young and didn't appear to be the sort who
would frown on living next door to the twins.

Of course, it didn't hurt that he was also very good
looking: tall, lean, blond and—she leaned forward to
get an even closer look at him—he had the most incredibly *blue* eyes behind that pair of gold wire-
rimmed glasses.

"I was thinking more of a half-gainer with a full
twist, myself. But I apologize if I scared you," she said
at last, smiling brightly as she pushed an errant lock
of long black hair away from her eyes. "But you can
relax. I haven't any plans for ending it all. At least not
this week. Did you really think I was going to fall?"

"The thought had crossed my mind," he answered, shading his eyes with one hand as he candidly returned her scrutiny. She felt suddenly warm, and extremely underdressed.

"Then I apologize again."

"And I accept again," he said, his open inspection of her bare legs decidedly unnerving. "I don't know if I should bring this up—but do you know you have a tube of glue stuck to your knee?"

"Do I know it?" Sydney exaggeratedly waggled her eyebrows as she clasped an invisible cigar close to her mouth. "Not really, but if you hum a few bars I think I can fake it," she quipped, then grinned as her audience of one laughed out loud, a distinctly appealing masculine sound. Oh yes, this man could prove to be a great neighbor.

She decided to pretend she didn't know he was Mrs. Harwick's summer tenant, just to see how much more she could learn about him. "Sorry, but I can never resist pulling out those old jokes. Marx Brothers movies turn me into a basket case. So, are you a daytripper or a weeker?"

"A what?" He frowned, pushing at the bridge of his glasses. "Oh—I think I understand. No, actually I'm a 'summer,' if such a term exists. I rented the upper floor of the house next door for the season. My name is Mansfield, by the way. Blake Mansfield. How long are you here for?" Sydney chuckled as he grimaced. "Lord, I should rephrase that, shouldn't I? It sounds like we're doing time on Alcatraz, not visiting Ocean City."

"Blake," she said, smiling inwardly. They'd only been talking for a minute and already she knew his name. His name, and the fact that his blue eyes sparkled with humor as well as intelligence—and a hint of sadness. "You'll be all alone, you know. Mrs. Harwick, who owns the house and lives downstairs year-round, has gone to visit her daughter and new grandchild in Pittsburgh until September."

"Yes, she did tell me that on the phone. Nice lady."

"A peach. She doesn't even mind the twins—which probably qualifies her for sainthood. Did you know Mrs. Harwick's place used to be a small boarding-house before she bought it and converted the upstairs to a rental condo? The previous owner had called it The Mallard Inn. And a real *ducky* place it was, Mrs. H says."

She watched as Blake laughed again, his beautiful blue eyes twinkling. She had long ago learned to rely on the accuracy of her first impressions and immediately decided to trust him. After all, ax murderers usually didn't sign summer leases.

"It seems as if we'll be neighbors for the duration. I'm Blackmun, by the by. Full name, Sydney Blackmun, if you want to get technical, which I certainly hope you won't. You can call me Sydney, or Syd, or anything else printable that may come to mind. I'm spending the summer converting this old pile into a bed-and-breakfast. They're the newest thing, you know."

She hopped to her feet, motioning toward the wooden steps. "And now that the introductions are out of the way, Blake—do you think you could possibly come up here and help me get this stupid tube of glue off my knee? I hate to admit it, but this stuff is beginning to sting.''

Chapter Two

"It's a good thing you bought the complete kit," Blake told Sydney fifteen minutes later as they sat together on the small, shady porch tucked onto the side of the first floor, sipping fresh homemade lemonade. "If it hadn't been for that solvent we might have had to amputate. I'm sure I have a rusty saw somewhere in my luggage."

"And a bullet for me to bite down on so that I wouldn't scream?" Sydney asked as she continued to dab a moist washcloth at her knee, which still looked red and a little sore. "Mom always taught me to be prepared." She glanced up at Blake. "Or could that be something I read last year when the twins were boning up on their scouting manual?"

She sat back in the old-fashioned wicker rocking chair and looked at him levelly. "Whatever, I'll give Herbie another go tomorrow, poor thing, once I buy another brand of glue. So, tell me—what do you do that you can take the entire summer off to laze away the days in Ocean City?''

Blake gave a slight shake of his head. The girl jumped from one subject to the other so quickly that he was sure a lesser man would already have begun to feel dizzy. As a matter of fact, he still wasn't quite sure how he had come to be sitting on this porch, surrounded by untidy heaps of badly chipped painted sections of porch railing, and sipping lemonade—a drink he had never particularly favored.

''I write,'' he heard himself answer, absently rubbing his right knee. ''Short stories, how-to's, anything I can to put food on the table. I've decided to try my hand at expanding one of my more successful stories into a play, and gave myself this summer to see if I can pull it off.''

Why had he told her that? He hadn't told anybody that. His plans were too private, too personal and too potentially painful if he failed and had to go back to supplementing his income with yet more stock articles on how to write a winning résumé.

''You're kidding!'' Sydney exploded, cutting short his thoughts. ''Boy, Ocean City's rapidly turning into a writers' retreat, isn't it?''

He waited while she took a long drink of her lemonade, watching her as her emerald green eyes seemed to sparkle with some secret knowledge. ''There are other writers here?''

''One. Well, not *here,* technically—not at the moment—although she does write most of her books while in Ocean City. She's on her second honeymoon at the moment, in Europe. Do you know the name Courtney Blackmun?''

Blake hesitated a moment, something in Sydney's tone challenging him. Wait a minute! Sydney had said her name was Blackmun. ''A relative of yours?'' he asked tentatively.

''Mother,'' she answered, pulling up her bare legs one after the other, to sit perched, lotus position, on the seat of the wicker chair. ''I hope you're suitably impressed. You have read her latest, haven't you?''

He'd barely had time to form an answer before she disappeared, barreling into the house, only to reappear a few seconds later with a paperback book in her hand.

''Here you go, Blake,'' she said, tossing the book into his lap. ''It's really great. Of course, *Questions of the Heart* will always be my personal favorite, for a lot of reasons, but this one's very good. Happy reading, and remember—there *will* be a quiz!

''Now, if you'll excuse me, I've got to go scrub some potatoes and stick them in the microwave. Plague and Pestilence will be swooping back in here any minute now, ready to gnaw on the furniture if I don't have supper ready for them. Or maybe I should put the meat loaf in first, and then the potatoes? Decisions, decisions. I don't know how anybody gets an entire meal onto the table at one time.''

Blake passed over the potato dilemma, knowing he wasn't qualified to give an opinion. ''Plague and Pestilence? You must mean the twins. I thought you said their names were Peter and Paul when you mentioned them while we were performing your 'glue-ectomy.' I think I met one of them on the sidewalk earlier. Which one is which?"

"I'm Plague, he's Pestilence," said a young male voice from the circular staircase that cut into the porch floor, leading up from the side yard. A second later a black-haired young boy had climbed onto the porch, his long, thin body covered head to foot with dried sand.

"No you're not. *I'm* Plague. *You're* Pestilence," corrected a second voice, as a carbon copy of the first boy—equally sand-covered—joined him on the porch, immediately heading for the iced jug of lemonade and the stack of paper cups sitting beside it. "Nobody was on the water when we got there, so we had a sand fight instead, in case you're wondering. I won." He turned back to his brother, placing two fingers behind his head as if they were Indian feathers. "How, Kemo Sabe. Me Plague—you Pestilence. When will you ever get that right, Paul?"

"What does it matter? It's all semantics, anyway, right, Syd? That's se-man-tics, Pete—three syllables. Do you think you can understand that one?" Paul accepted a cup of lemonade from his brother and drained it in one long gulp. "Phew! That's better. Thanks. Hello," he said at last, looking at Blake. "You're the guy I nearly ran into a little while ago, aren't you? What are you doing here?"

"Oh, good, Paul, real good," Pete broke in, wiping his hand on his swim trunks before extending it to Blake. "And you're supposed to be the polite one. Mom would have kittens if she heard you. Let me show you how it's done."

Blake took Pete's hand, feeling the grit of sand against his palm as the two of them exchanged the formal greeting.

"Hello, sir," Pete said. "My name is Peter Richardson. I'm extremely honored to meet you. Please excuse my brother. When he was two he fell out of his crib onto his head."

Paul held out his equally sandy hand next, grinning widely as he maneuvred his brother out of the way. "Look who's talking. He pushed me, you know," he said, gripping Blake's hand firmly. "I'm sorry if I was rude. How do you do, sir?"

Sydney stepped in to complete the introductions while Blake looked back and forth between the two boys, amazed by their two-peas-in-a-pod appearance. "How do you tell them apart?" he asked at last, once the twins had retreated to chairs on the far side of the porch, amicably arguing the qualities of two brands of basketball sneakers.

"It isn't easy," she admitted, refilling his glass before he could tell her he'd already had enough. "But Paul has a small crescent-shaped scar at the outside corner of his right eye, so that helps."

"Which is probably why she beaned him with that ball in the first place. See, I'm not the only one. The whole family can be very big on violence," Pete put in before returning to his argument of the merits of neon green high-tops that blew themselves up over "that generic junk."

"All three of you look very much alike, now that I've had time to consider it," Blake commented to Sydney, automatically taking another sip of lemonade. "Same hair. Same emerald green eyes. Yet you have different last names."

Sydney nodded, seemingly not upset by his interest. "You caught that, did you? Mom married Adam Richardson—New Jersey's senior senator, if you're wondering where you heard that name before—when I was thirteen. Nine months later—boom! None of our lives have been the same since. You have any brothers or sisters?"

"No, I'm an only child," he replied absently, still intent on trying to tell Pete from Paul. It wasn't as if he'd never seen twins before, but these twins were almost uncannily similar. "What do you do when they're wearing sunglasses—or after dark? I mean, they seem so alike. You'd have to have more than an old war wound to guide you."

"Oh, we have our ways." Sydney called to her brothers. "Hey, I need some help here, guys. Pete— why don't you tell Blake what you want to be when you grow up."

"You mean this week?" Paul shot back, grinning.

"Stuff it, Paul," Pete answered automatically and without anger before turning to his sister. "Ace relief pitcher for the New York Yankees ball club. They need all the help they can get, you know."

"Last week he wanted to join the Peace Corps and build bridges in Ecuador," Sydney whispered to Blake out of the corner of her mouth. "And now you, Paul. Tell Blake about the burning desire that has been with you since nursery school."

Paul looked at Blake, no hint of a smile in his eyes. "I'm going to be president of the United States," he said with such conviction that Blake wasn't even tempted to question him. "As a country, we also need all the help we can get."

Sydney rose from her chair and took a slight bow. "I rest my case, sir. They may look alike, but each is his own person, bless both their bloodthirsty little hearts. Now, much as I'm enjoying this, I have to get supper on the table. Will you join us?"

"Not unless he has a death wish, he won't," Pete teased in a stage whisper to Paul, who rolled his eyes and grabbed at his midsection as if he had suddenly taken ill.

"*Um*—I think not. Not tonight," Blake answered as Sydney stuck out her tongue at her brothers. He liked Sydney and the twins, but this was getting too chummy too fast. He was here for work, not fun. "I still have a lot of unpacking to do. But thanks for asking." He turned to the boys and winked. "And thanks for the warning."

The twins were instantly on their feet. "Want some help?"

Blake looked at the two sand-covered bodies, sensing their eagerness to help. There was a difference between being chummy and accepting an offer of simple courtesy. Besides, it had been a long drive and he would be grateful for the help. "Why not?" He reached into his pants pocket and drew out the keys to his car, tossing them to the nearest twin. "Just pile the stuff on the landing outside the door. I'll take it from there."

"Good deal. And we'll be up on the boardwalk tonight around eight-thirty for pizza at the stand across from the Music Pier,'' Pete volunteered, winking at his brother as they headed for the spiral staircase. ''Maybe you'll want to treat each of us to a slice, just to thank us for carrying your stuff? Syd will be with us.''

''Peter!'' Sydney frowned.

''Jerk,'' Paul gibed, giving his brother a small shove. ''And you talked about my manners?''

The boy raised his hands in self-defense. ''Hey, give me a break. I was only planning ahead. You said Sydney promised us frozen yogurt, but I hadn't heard anything about pizza.''

''I'm sorry about that, Blake. Hollow legs, the two of them,'' Sydney told Blake brightly as she followed him down the circular staircase and onto the pavement. ''If they don't eat every two hours they begin to rattle when they walk. And please ignore their so-subtle matchmaking instincts. They figure if I'm busy being romanced I won't have time to put paintbrushes in their hands.''

Blake looked at her quizzically. ''You're going to put paintbrushes in their hands? Talk about your death wishes—I hope you've got plenty of insurance on this place.''

She grinned at his joke. ''I have great faith in them, really. We're going to start putting a base coat on the main porch tomorrow, now that the workmen have gotten it all sanded and primed. Herbert showed up as a momentary diversion, although he's going to make a great watchdog. I've got to get back down to some serious work or otherwise Mom will come home from

Europe to hang an I-told-you-so sign around my neck.
She said I'd never get it all done in three months.''

"So that's why there's no railing around the front
porch," Blake said as they walked to the front of the
large four-story Victorian clapboard house and the
sight of the immense porch that wrapped halfway
around the building above the brick ground floor.
"Those were the balustrades I saw piled up on the side
porch, weren't they? It looks like you've really got
your work cut out for you."

Sydney laughed, putting her hands on her hips.
"That's an understatement. There are dozens of those
balustrades, each holding a half dozen spindles, or
balusters—I'm really adding to my vocabulary this
summer—and each of them needs to be stripped of at
least three coats of old paint. I couldn't bear to re-
place them with reproductions when the originals look
so gorgeous, so I'm going to have them dipped—I
think that's the term. Then I'll paint them before the
carpenters reattach them to the porch."

Blake looked up at the immense clapboard house
that showed signs of both the saltwater air and years
of neglect. He'd already had a glimpse of the interior
as they passed through the first floor to reach the side
porch. The new spackled drywall, unpainted door,
floor and ceiling moldings and stripped hardwood
floors in every room were all in need of finishing. "I
think your mother's right, Sydney. It'll take you more
than a single summer to turn this place into a profit-
able enterprise."

Sydney looked up at the front facade, her green eyes
glowing with pride. "Ah, but then you don't know me

very well, do you? Just give me three months and you won't know the place.''

She turned to face him, and he felt his stomach do a small, involuntary flip at the sight of her animated face. "Pops has already dubbed the place *Sydney's Folly*. Great name, huh? But I'll prove them wrong, both he and Mom. Just you wait and see. Sydney's Folly will be the best little bed-and-breakfast in Ocean City."

Seven hours later, alone in her first-floor bedroom, the romantic light of a full moon shining through the windows and onto her folding cot, Sydney tried to ignore her aching limbs and the slight stinging sensation that still emanated from her left knee.

It had been another long day, broken only by Blake Mansfield's unexpected appearance, and she knew herself to be nearly exhausted, although her mind remained blindingly awake.

Funny that Blake hadn't shown up on the boardwalk, even though he had told the boys they might have to give him a rain check on the pizza because he was too tired to make any promises.

His absence had put a damper on the evening for her, so that she had barely enjoyed beating the twins at a game of miniature golf at their favorite boardwalk course, sinking only three holes-in-one on the front nine.

She turned onto her side, looking through the uncurtained window at the ceiling light that still burned in Blake's second-floor apartment. Land was at a premium in Ocean City, so that houses were built on

long, narrow patches of ground, and the side wall of
Mrs. Harwick's house couldn't be more than twenty
feet away from her window.

Sydney had been dressing in the bathroom ever
since she moved in, not planning to concentrate on
decorating the bedrooms for a while, but now that she
had a neighbor she had better start thinking about at
least putting up curtains.

Her mind dismissed that thought and skipped effortlessly on to another. It was getting very late. Surely
Blake had finished unpacking by now, even if he had
spent part of the evening laying in a supply of grocer-
ies.

Could he be burning the midnight wattage working
on his play? Or maybe he had begun reading her
mother's latest book. That should keep him up all
night, she thought smugly.

Her mother. Sydney collapsed onto her back once
more, thinking about her wonderful, long-suffering
mother.

At twenty-five, Sydney had finally called a halt to
her formal education, having completed both college
and graduate school before travelling to England for
an additional year of specialized study.

When Sydney had come home to New Jersey in
mid-April, she hadn't made any bones about the fact
that, after a lifetime spent learning, she and her brain
needed to take a well-deserved vacation! She was, she
had told them, all "schooled out."

Her parents had been pleased—right after Courtney had threatened to take her daughter's tempera-
ture—accustomed as they were to a Sydney who had

spent her first twenty-five years seemingly madly
rushing in six directions at once, including doggedly
working at odd jobs every summer to help pay for her
own tuition.

After only three short weeks spent dedicatedly trying to become addicted to chocolate-covered ice-cream
bars and lying on the couch watching daytime soap
operas, Sydney had traveled with Courtney, Adam
and the twins to their condo in Ocean City to begin a
leisurely family summer vacation—and that's when it
happened.

While taking the family Labrador, Pundit, for a
long walk, she had stumbled across the vacant Victorian house at the corner of Delancey Place and Co-
rinthian Avenue. She had immediately fallen in love
with the huge, homely, faintly run-down building.
And within a heartbeat, inspiration—almost divine
inspiration, according to Sydney—had struck.

It was perfect! Well, maybe not perfect, but it was
much better than lounging on the couch, eating ice
cream and watching her hips widen. Without telling
anyone, she used part of her trust fund to put a down
payment on the house, planning to turn it into a bed-
and-breakfast.

The same day her application for a mortgage had
been approved she had announced her plans, including one slight addition she had thought up while waiting to hear from the bank. This addition became the
"divine" part of her inspiration. She would enlist Paul
and Pete as her helpers, allowing her parents to go on
an extended and most definitely well-deserved second
honeymoon.

"And this house will only be the first," Sydney remembered boasting as Adam and Courtney had stood on the cracked pavement in front of the run-down building, listening indulgently. "There have to be literally *tons* of old houses like it in Ocean City, in Cape May—all up and down the coast. I can redo a new one every summer. I've stayed in a million hotels, you know, so I know all about them. Besides, how difficult could it be?"

"How difficult, indeed? Thirty days of enjoying myself watching Sydney doing nothing," Adam had said to his wife, shaking his head as he eyed the peeling paint on the upstairs dormer. "Did we really believe she could go through an entire summer without taking on some sort of project? We should have known it was too good to last."

Then, smiling, he kissed his wife's cheek. "Tell me, darling, how does Paris sound to you?"

And so, armed with her usual optimistic enthusiasm, her parents' cautious blessings—and precious little conception of what she might really be getting herself into—Sydney had happily plunged ahead.

Yet, so far everything was going along swimmingly, she decided as she stretched her toes toward the bottom of the cot.

Her mother and Adam had departed for their second honeymoon, leaving the twins with Sydney.

The house, wearing a new roof, and completely rewired and fitted out with new walls, plumbing and all that mundane, uninteresting stuff—details she had agreed to leave to experts—was actually beginning to take shape.

Now all she had to do was paint the inside of the place, decorate it, furnish it, hang out her sign, then stand back and watch while the paying customers beat a path to her door.

Of course, convincing the boys to stay in Delancey Place rather than the comfortable condo hadn't been easy, but since the project had the air of camping out, she had finally convinced them that only the overindulged and chickenhearted would stay over three miles away at the family condo when endless adventure waited for them in Delancey Place.

Sydney cupped her hands behind her head, smiling up at the ceiling light in the house next door. Yes, things were progressing quite nicely so far, right down to the requisite handsome, eligible man next door. All in all, this just might prove to be one of the most memorable summers in her life.

Chapter Three

Blake had dropped fully clothed onto his bed a little before nine, with lights still burning throughout the condo, promising himself he was only going to rest his eyes for a few minutes. He awoke just before dawn, startled to discover himself in unfamiliar surroundings and vaguely unsettled by the memory of a dream in which a black-haired, emerald-eyed mermaid had figured prominently.

An hour later, showered, dressed and finishing the remains of a freshly made glazed doughnut he had bought at a small stand on the boardwalk, he walked down the wooden stairs onto the deserted beach just as the sun began to rise above the water, throwing a warm pink blush over sky, sea and sand.

He stopped on the second step from the bottom, shading his eyes as he watched the waves gently breaking far from shore, the only whitecaps to be seen being those that hit against the stone jetties that jutted into the ocean at irregular intervals up and down the length of the beach.

To his left, eight miles away and barely visible through the early morning haze, stood the tall hotels and gambling casinos of Atlantic City. The faraway scene looked unearthly, like some vague, garish photograph of another world, a world he had left behind and didn't really miss.

Smiling, he wondered briefly if he had the makings of a beach bum locked inside himself somewhere. But no, he had come here to work. Playing was for people who didn't have to find a way to live from one magazine-article sale to the next.

Which didn't mean he couldn't enjoy at least one day away from his typewriter, did it?

The sand felt cool beneath his bare feet as he began walking toward the sea. Deep inside him, Blake felt his taut nerves and muscles begin to relax. Yes, this might just do it; this seaside town, this peace, this much-needed change of scenery. In this place, and with a little bit of luck, he just might be able to pull it off.

As gulls screamed above his head and gentle wavelets ran up the sand to lick at his feet, the memory of Sydney Blackmun sprang, unbidden, to his mind.

She could present a problem for him in this small corner of paradise, she and her twin brothers. Blake hadn't counted on taking the time to get to know his neighbors, but he already knew it would be as impossible for him to ignore Sydney as it would be for him to turn back the incoming tide. She just wasn't the ignorable type.

Blake was suddenly aware that he was no longer alone on the beach. A tallish black-haired female figure dressed head to bare toes in a silky white jogging outfit that the slight breeze blew against her slim, enticing form, was running toward him.

Well, not actually toward him. Hers was more of a meandering path, broken by slight detours as she chased the wavelets back into the ocean or turned in circles, her arms outstretched as she seemed to chatter amicably with the seagulls.

It was Sydney, just as if the thought of her had somehow conjured her up. Blake watched, entranced, as she bent to pick up several very small stones and slip them into her pocket before unzipping her jacket and removing it to reveal a skintight emerald-green spandex tank top. Only as she was tying the jacket around her waist by its sleeves as she walked up the beach did she seem to notice him.

"Blake!" she exclaimed, waving as she scampered through a miniature tide pool to reach his side. "Isn't it a glorious day? The beach is always dressed in its company best early in the morning. You look well rested. That's a glazed doughnut, isn't it? Did you get it on the boardwalk? They make them fresh every morning, you know. It's nearly impossible to walk by, smell them and not buy any. So softly fresh and very sinfully sugary. *Yum.*"

She looked pointedly at the waxed white bag he was carrying and then up at him, smiling wickedly. "Don't you have any more in there, or were you just planning to make me beg?"

"Begging's good," Blake heard himself answer, his mind already fairly well occupied in watching the sun play against the shiny emerald spandex with each breath she took. "Although I've always preferred abject groveling, myself."

"So you have a mean streak, do you?" Sydney commented, arching one finely sculpted brow. "No wonder the boys took to you on sight."

He reached into the bag and pulled out the cream-filled powdered doughnut he had bought on impulse, planning to enjoy it later with his coffee when he returned to the condo. "Here, I never could stand to see a child go hungry."

Sydney accepted it greedily. "Oh, thank you, kind sir. But I'd rather go up onto the boardwalk to eat it. Showing food this close to those gulls always turns the place into an attack scene from *The Birds*." She began walking toward the stairs, stopping only to scoop up a pair of high-topped sneakers he hadn't noticed lying on the sand.

Blake sat on a nearby bench while Sydney, dropping gracefully to sit on the boardwalk, used her wrinkled socks to brush sand from her feet, then tugged on the socks. As she was tying her second sneaker she peeped at Blake out of the corner of her eyes. "So, did you get any reading done last night?" she asked, smiling up at him.

Blake shook his head as he got up, reaching down a hand to pull Sydney to her feet. "Sorry. I wanted to, but I took a ten-hour nap instead." Turning, they both began walking down the boardwalk. "I didn't even eat supper before I passed out, now that I think of it."

Sydney, who had almost gotten the doughnut to her lips, stopped in her tracks. "Here," she said, offering him the pastry. "You must be starving."

"Thanks—hey!"

Just as quickly as she had offered the doughnut, she took it away. "No! You can't fill up on doughnuts. They're just empty calories. Great-tasting calories— but empty. Trust me on this. You're talking to a woman who tried to exist on chocolate-covered ice-cream bars for nearly a month. Come on, Blake, I know a great Italian restaurant near the Music Pier. A couple of eggs, some home fries, toast and bacon, and you'll be ready to lick the world."

"Home-fried potatoes in an Italian restaurant?" Blake shook his head. "Do you think I could have a side order of spaghetti? I'm really hungry."

"Nut!" Sydney said shaking her head. "Although the spaghetti is delicious."

She took his hand and began pulling him down the ramp that led to Delancey Place. "You can borrow one of the twin's bikes and we'll ride up to the restaurant. They always promise to get up with me to watch the sun rise, but they haven't made it yet. You'll love riding on the boardwalk. We can only do it until eleven o'clock, of course, but then there have to be rules or else there would be anarchy. At least, that's what Pops told the boys when they got caught trying to take their bikes on the boardwalk after eleven."

Blake felt himself being carried along by the sheer force of Sydney's excitement and wondered if it really was against his will. He smiled, already knowing the answer. He had never done anything against his will.

Nothing, that is, except to give up the one thing in his life that had mattered to him most.

"Pops," he echoed, as they made their way to the rear of the Victorian house and the small storage barn that stood against the back fence. "What sort of name is that for the senior senator from New Jersey?"

Sydney turned to him, and he noticed that her lips were lightly dusted with powdered sugar. When had she had time to devour the doughnut? "I used to call him Adam when he and Mom were first married. I worried that Mom might think I was being disrespectful to my real father if I had called Adam Dad. But then Mom took me aside about six months after the wedding to tell me that Adam had no intention of trying to take my father's place. He just wanted to love me—which was why he had grounded me for staying out past my curfew. That seemed like a loving, parent-type reaction to me. Well, I was watching this old movie later that night—one of those down-home Andy Hardy things—and the girl in the movie called her father Pops. I ran it past Mom and she thought it was cute. Adam has been Pops to me ever since."

By the time Sydney had completed this long story the two of them were walking their bikes back to the boardwalk.

"You know what, Sydney?" Blake offered, pushing his bike ahead of him up the ramp. "I would have hated to find you on the other end of the line while I was working part-time as a telephone interviewer in college. I would have asked one question and gotten a chapter-length answer. Tell me, Ms. Blackmun," he said in a parody of such a conversation, "what is your opinion of the country's chances of balancing the trade deficit within this century? Good? Fair? Poor?" He shook his head. "I have a feeling the century would end before your answer did."

"I do talk a lot, don't I?" Sydney answered, flashing him a grin that told him he hadn't insulted her. "And I say too much as well, or at least Pops says so. Up until a few years ago he refused to discuss his work with me, saying my mouth was a national security risk."

Blake laughed out loud. "I'll have to remember that." He slung one long leg over the bicycle to sit on the thin banana seat, his feet planted firmly on the boardwalk as he watched Sydney mount her own bike. "I'm starving. Lead me to my Italian breakfast. I think I need some solid food."

"Grazie, signore. A presto!" Sydney waved to the smiling man who daily sat outside his restaurant greeting everyone who walked past as she and Blake mounted their bicycles and headed back down the boardwalk toward Delancey Place. "Oh, I'm stuffed to the gills," she said, patting her flat stomach. "Next time it's my treat. Now, where were we? Oh, yes—the Civil War. What general were we up to before the waitress reminded us that we'd have to get our bicycles off the boardwalk before eleven?"

"Burnside," Blake answered, immediately launching into a recitation of the man's running battles with Lincoln as they leisurely pedalled past joggers and surreys, while young children played tag in the center of the boardwalk and sea gulls fought over scraps of food tossed to them by people sitting on benches overlooking the beach.

Sydney listened with only half an ear, content to watch Blake's face as he continued the discussion that had lasted them through a leisurely breakfast and two extra cups of coffee. He certainly was a knowledgeable man, she thought, but he wasn't like some people she had known, who seemed to enjoy beating other people over the head with their intelligence.

"So, when Lincoln felt he'd had enough, he replaced the last one with Ulysses S. Grant," Sydney said when it seemed like it was her turn to speak once more, "and the rest is history!"

"*All* of it is history, when you get right down to it," Blake joked as he led the way off the boardwalk and onto Delancey Place. "Uh-oh. Here come the twins, and they don't look happy. Do you think we should have left them a note?"

Sydney looked up the street to see her brothers advancing on them, their faces twisted into murderous scowls. "Uh-oh is right. They don't look very happy, do they? I wonder if—Blake, quick—what's today's date?"

She didn't really need to hear his answer, for she already knew what she had forgotten. Today was the day before the big kite-flying contest at the recreation field, and she had promised to take the boys kite shopping this morning. How could she have forgotten something so important?

Sydney pulled a face at her own question. How? That wasn't the proper thing to ask. The real question was *who?* Now, that was a question for which there could be only one answer. She had forgotten the boys the moment she had seen Blake on the beach, looking bemused, rather lost, a little overwhelmed, and still so terribly, terribly handsome.

It was amazing how a man who stood a good ten inches higher than her own five feet eight inches could make her want to take him in her arms and tell him everything was going to be all right. Not that he appeared the least bit timid or shy. It wasn't that at all. It was just a certain way he had of carrying his head, and a small, sad cast to his beautiful blue eyes, that told her that Blake Mansfield hadn't so much *come* to Ocean City as he had *run* to it. And she was going to find out why!

"Syd!"

Sydney snapped herself out of her private thoughts at the sound of Pete's voice. "Hi, guys," she said, grimacing. "Decided not to sleep till noon today, huh? So, did you eat?"

Pete walked up to her, flattening his palms on either side of the handlebars. He leaned his head close to hers, his jaw jutting forward in belligerence, while his emerald eyes spat green fire. "Paul heated some of those frozen breakfast things you bought in the microwave," he told her through gritted teeth. "The pancakes weighed ten pounds apiece and the bacon was soggy."

"I did not buy those frozen breakfast things in the microwave, Pete," Sydney replied, less intent on correcting her brother's grammar than she was in stalling for time. "I bought them in the store. You were incorrectly modifying—"

Pete pulled a face. "Ah, come on. It's summertime. Lighten up, okay?"

Sydney nodded. "Point well made, Pete. But if you've reverted to caveman grunts by September, it won't be on my head."

"Syd!"

It seemed it was Paul's turn to talk, and she turned to look at him. "Yes, master? You bellowed?"

"Do you have any idea what day this is?" her brother asked, although his tone made his question sound more like an accusation.

Her smile was wide and meant to dazzle. "Do I know what day this is? Oh, how you wound me. Of course I know. It's the day before the kite-flying contest, and we're leaving for the hobby store in—" she consulted her watch "—exactly five minutes. I'm hurt, guys, really crushed, that you'd think I could forget anything so important."

She looked over at Blake, silently conveying the message that she believed he could at least applaud her convincing lie.

Paul, whose wooden expression told her that one of her brothers remained unconvinced, began nodding his head in a maddeningly knowing way that made Sydney aware that if the boy decided against the presidency, he'd make a great prosecuting attorney. "I see," he said consideringly. "So you didn't forget the kites. Then may we assume that you also did not forget that today's the day you told Mr. O'Reilly it was all right for him to come over from Somers Point to show you how to work those power tools?"

"Power tools?" Blake questioned, laughing, "Whoa, fellas—time out! She's going to use power tools? Maybe you guys ought to rethink this kite business to stay home and sell tickets—after you check the first-aid cabinet. She did tell you about the glue, didn't she?" Blake's tone was openly skeptical of her ability to master a simple mechanical device, which was the only thing that kept Sydney from groaning aloud, for she had completely forgotten nice old Mr. O'Reilly.

"I'm not going to be using a jigsaw or anything like that," she told him reasonably, resisting the impulse to stick out her tongue at him. "Just a small power spray-painter for the walls and some little thingama-bob for the woodwork. And, no," she continued, looking straight at Paul as she fibbed, "I did not forget that Mr. O'Reilly is due here in less than ten minutes, which you would have known if you had waited for me to tell you what I've planned, rather than jumping on me like a couple of distrusting schoolmistresses who will live forever in my memory."

"Oh, yeah?" This came from Pete, who had just nudged his brother in the side. "If you have a plan, let's hear it. *Now*. Paul and I wanted to win that contest this year."

"Yeah, Syd," Paul echoed his brother. "Let's hear this great plan of yours."

Sydney looked to Blake, as if for help. Plan? Why did they have to ask her for her plan? She didn't have a plan. What she had was a big mouth! All she could hope for now was some sort of divine intervention!

She smiled evilly. *Blake*. Yes. Blake would help her. "*Um*—Blake?"

His amused gaze slid away from hers. "Yeah, well, I think I hear my mother calling me." Blake pushed his bike forward as if to make good his escape. "Yup— there she goes again. You heard her, didn't you, guys? See you later, Sydney."

"Blake has agreed to take you!" Sydney blurted before he could get away. "No one can ever work on their very first day in Ocean City. Even Mom can't, and she has been coming here for years. Besides, he knows positively *everything* there is to know about kites—don't you, Blake?"

Chapter Four

The cloudless sky was filled with kites of every color, size and description. There were ferocious Japanese dragons. There were kites designed to look like every comic-book hero to ever hit the commercial trail. There were old-fashioned box kites and kites with tails that seemed half as long as the football field they sailed above in the stiff breeze that came inland from the ocean.

And then there was one kite that totally defied description—not that everyone didn't give it a good try anyway.

Paul said it reminded him of something he once saw in his advanced science class.

Pete contended that it was a takeoff of one of Salvador Dali's melting pocket watches.

Sydney tried to explain it from another angle, saying that the kite didn't have to resemble any one thing

in particular—it just had to make "a statement."
Which it most certainly did.

It was left to Blake to name the loving-hands-at-
home creation, concocted from pieces of several different kite kits. He dubbed it Soap on a Rope, and the
name stuck.

Soap on a Rope took second prize for originality,
and although the twins protested privately that they
should have taken the grand prize "just for getting the
stupid thing to stay in the air in the first place," Blake
was lauded as a hero at the celebratory lunch Sydney
treated them to at the Italian restaurant.

Pete was still nursing his wounds. "I can't believe
they gave the top prize to a kite shaped like a pagoda!
It wasn't fair that those girls ordered it all the way
from some place out west, either. Our kite was home-
grown."

Paul nodded his agreement, adding, "The worst of
it is that they're younger than we are. It stinks losing
to girls in the first place, but when they're ten and
seven, it's downright embarrassing!"

"I think the worst part is that they wouldn't tell you
the name of the kite company they ordered it from. I
did hear you asking them, you know. Now, would it
be rude of me," Sydney asked, leaning her elbows on
the table, "if I were to point out that you're both being terribly chauvinistic, on top of sounding like pretty
rotten sports? And I haven't heard you thank Blake
yet for all his hard work. Shame on you."

The boys quickly apologized to both Blake and their
sister.

"That's all right, boys," Sydney said while they were waiting for their food. "You'll get them next time. What is it next week? The sand-sculpting contest? I bet Blake will love it."

"Wrong. Blake will be too busy doing what he came here to do to love it," Blake corrected, reaching for a piece of crusty garlic bread. "I got roped into the kite contest in a moment of weakness. This one's on you, Sydney."

She opened her mouth to protest, then wisely closed it. It was enough that Blake and the twins had spent the best part of yesterday together in the backyard putting the kite together, and all this morning running up and down the football field with their ugly masterpiece.

Blake's fair skin had begun to show signs of having been in the sun, and the clouded look she had seen in his eyes upon his arrival had definitely started to clear. He smiled more, seemed to actually enjoy the twins, and had agreed to come to lunch with them. That was as far as Sydney had originally been prepared to go in her Mary Poppins routine.

He had helped her, first with that stupid tube of glue, and then with the kite. She, in return, had shown him some fun; helped him remember that Ocean City wasn't just a good place to work on his play. The score was even.

From now on, it was going to have to be up to Blake to make the moves.

He was interesting, and she liked him, but she wasn't about to make him into one of what her family, sometimes laughingly, sometimes while shaking in their boots, called "Sydney's projects."

But he *was* interesting. She *did* like him. And he was *so* appealing. She smiled into her napkin. Well, maybe she'd help him a little bit more, but only if it looked like he needed a gentle nudge in the right direction.

Sydney laughed as Paul made a joke, and took a quick peek at Blake out of the corner of her eye. His smile was a wonder, and his laugh deep and unaffected. She hadn't known a man could wear glasses and still be so dangerously attractive. And then there was that vulnerable, slightly sad look in his eyes. *Very* intriguing. Perhaps it was time she got back to concentrating on her new house, before she found herself getting in too deep.

For if one thing was already certain to Sydney, it was that Blake Mansfield wasn't in the market for a summertime romance.

Putting his typewriter on the desk in front of one of the living-room windows had been his first mistake. His second mistake had been lifting his attention from the page and looking out that window to see Sydney painting her front porch.

From that moment, and for nearly every moment he'd spent at the desk the two succeeding days, the typewriter and his work had been forgotten.

There ought to be a law, he told himself, a law forbidding such long, straight legs, or such brief, revealing shorts. And tank tops, once the uncontested domain of men, had no business on women whose body contours strained at the curve-hugging ribbed cotton cloth.

Her only concession to the job at hand was the oversized white painter's cap she wore at a jaunty angle, all her gorgeous black hair tucked up inside it so that she looked little more than a child as she stuck out her tongue while stretching to reach the top of one of the posts with her brush.

Couldn't she have found a sturdier ladder than that ancient wooden thing that looked as if it were held together by electrical tape and some kindly god whose job it was to protect imbeciles from their own foolhardiness?

Every time she had climbed it, Blake had been convinced the thing was going to splinter as she hung onto it with one hand while reaching toward the top of one of the half dozen columns that lined the edge of the porch.

The twins had been painting with her for a while this morning, until Paul had nearly stepped in a can of paint and Pete had accidentally—Blake knew he was being charitable in terming the move accidental—mistaken his brother's left arm for a column and painted it from shoulder to wrist.

Sydney had quickly confiscated their brushes and sent them to the beach, a move that had the boys skipping down the street five minutes later, exchanging high-fives and not appearing in the least repentant.

She had continued with the job alone, her only companion a portable compact-disc player that had belted out pulsating pop songs while the twins were there but now showcased a selection of Andrew Lloyd Webber show tunes. As the songs had played and Blake had watched, Sydney's body language and brush strokes mimicked the pace and flow of the music, and her unselfconscious vocal accompaniment of one tongue-twisting song from *Cats* had nearly made him laugh out loud.

As he continued his observation of her—refusing to give what he was doing any other name—Sydney turned her head toward the house as if she had heard something, then disappeared from sight.

"Probably the telephone," Blake told himself, looking down to see that the page in the typewriter was still completely blank. "Talk about being saved by the bell. Thank you, Alexander, or I'd never get any work done today."

He picked up his notes, scanning them for some previously hidden hint of inspiration. The short story had been good, very good, but it hadn't contained enough substance to fill the longer length of a play. And it hadn't really had a resolution, a real ending. Modern short stories didn't have to contain a real ending. They just existed, like slices out of time. A serious stage play was another matter entirely. He had to add to the story, embellish it without padding it, and bring the protagonist to some sort of reasonable, workable conclusion. Maybe he could give the protagonist a love interest?

He picked up the magazine containing his short story and read over the lines he had highlighted, areas he had thought could be developed into entire scenes. Ten minutes later he threw down the magazine, his mind turned to figurative mush. A love interest? Where had he come up with that asinine idea?

He couldn't think about the play. He couldn't think about separate scenes. All he could think about was the way Sydney looked as she bent from the waist to reload her brush in the bucket that sat on the porch floor. All he had been able to think about for almost three days was Sydney.

"Damn!" He ripped the empty sheet of paper from the typewriter and mashed it into a ball before tossing it, overhand, into the wastebasket. "Swish. Two points. The buzzer sounds, ending the game. And the crowd roars. The team hoists Mansfield to its shoulders and carries him off the floor!"

Blake dropped his head into his hands, ruefully laughing at himself. "Mansfield, get a grip. This is getting you nowhere."

He looked out the window again, not knowing if he wanted to see Sydney or if he hoped she had quit for the day. "What the—?" Sydney had returned to the porch, all right. And she was looking up at him, her lips moving as she excitedly motioned for him to come down.

Something must be wrong! She'd had a telephone call and there was a problem with her parents or perhaps with the twins. Rather than waste time opening the window to hear her, Blake turned and made a beeline for the door, running down the outside staircase and across the lawn to the porch.

"You had a telephone call. What's the matter? Who's hurt?" he asked, taking the porch steps two at a time.

Sydney's quick warning stopped him just as he had been about to step into the paint bucket. "Hurt?" she questioned, looking at him as if he had suddenly sprouted broccoli from his ears. "Oh, you thought that—well, of course you did. How stupid of me. No. Nobody's hurt. I just spent five minutes on the phone with some guy trying to sell me land in Florida, or a cemetery plot, or something. I don't really remember, but he was very nice. He lives in a small town in Missouri, and he's working his way through college selling—"

"Syd, for crying out loud!" Blake interrupted, rapidly losing his temper. "I don't care if he's working his way through reform school. *What* do you want?"

"Well, actually," she answered, not appearing the least bit cowed by his show of anger, "while I was on the phone I happened to look up at the clock and saw that it was nearly lunchtime, which explained the way my stomach was grumbling the whole time I was on the phone. Anyway, since you have to eat as well, and because I forgot to go to the store this morning, I was wondering if you'd like to take a break and go for pizza on the boardwalk."

Blake felt his blood beginning to boil. "That's it? You're hungry? I thought there was something wrong!"

Sydney put out a hand to touch his arm, her sympathetic smile blighting him. "I know that, Blake, and I'm sorry. Please forgive me."

He raised his hands, then dropped them, giving up the fight. Yelling at Sydney for being impetuous was like spanking a puppy for wagging its tail. "I forgive you. Now, is there anything else?"

"Yes, as a matter of fact, there is. I can't go up on the boardwalk looking like this." She spread her hands, as if inviting him to inspect her paint-spattered clothes. He did, against his will, and felt his anger receding even further, to be replaced by another feeling he didn't believe it would be healthy for him to examine at any length. "Anyway, I really need to have you locate Plague and Pestilence on the beach while I hop in the shower, and then we can all go to lunch together."

She tipped her head to one side, smiling up at him as he watched a small dimple appear near the corner of her mouth. "You wouldn't mind hunting up the boys for me, would you?"

He didn't know whether he wanted to kill her or kiss her. She was playing the innocent, but he felt sure they both knew she was enjoying herself immensely. Blake closed his eyes, willing his heart to return to its normal steady rhythm. "Sydney," he said at last, sighing. "I know this might not be the best time to ask this question, but do you happen to remember my telling you that I came to Ocean City to *work?*"

Pulling off her cap so that her long black hair tumbled around her shoulders, Sydney shook her head and airily replied, "Nope. I don't remember that for a moment. But now that you mention it, you've been sitting up there at your desk all morning, staring out the window, just as you did yesterday and the day before that. You might want to move it—the desk, that is. Mom always makes sure her desk faces a blank wall or else, she says, her mind will be distracted. So, Blake," Sydney continued, grinning widely, "exactly how much work have you gotten done since we saw you last?"

Her words made up his mind for him. He wanted to kill her. All that dancing and prancing, and those skimpy outfits—how much of it had been for his benefit? Blake narrowed his eyes, then pushed at the bridge of his glasses. "Let me get this straight. You *knew* I could see you?"

Her grin widened, if such a thing was possible. "Every minute," she admitted, her emerald eyes large and innocent.

Blake looked down at her for a long time; looked down into her smiling face, then all the way down her slim form to her toes before raising his eyes once more to her face. "You ought to come with a warning label, Sydney," he said at last.

She shook her head, grimacing. "I know you've never read any of my mother's books, but are you sure you never met her? She says that all the time."

He ignored her and turned for the steps. "I'll go get the boys. But when we get back, you'd better have some clothes on. You got that?"

"Yes, sir!" Sydney responded, clicking her bare heels together and executing a smart salute.

Blake had just reached the pavement when she called to him. He turned around to see her standing on the porch, her tanned arms wrapped around one of the thick wooden pillars, one foot lazily swinging back and forth in the air as she leaned out over the edge. "What do you want now?"

She rested her cheek against the freshly painted wood. "Just one thing, Blake," she answered softly. "It's Ocean City in the summer. It's a warm, beautiful, sunshiny day. So, like Pete said—lighten up, okay?"

What he didn't hear as he set off down the pavement, muttering under his breath, was Sydney saying encouragingly to herself as she skipped into the house, "If the mountain won't come to Muhammad—"

Chapter Five

There was no getting around it. Sydney Blackmun was on the lookout for a summer romance—and she had already picked out her victim. *Him.* Blake knew it. And he was pretty sure Sydney was delightedly aware that he knew it.

She had very obligingly taken a verbal backseat during lunch, while he and the twins discussed the Yankees' chances for a pennant, and Blake was grateful for her consideration, while at the same time sure that he would be made to pay for her "kindness" later.

Once lunch was over, Blake, Sydney and the twins walked along the boardwalk taking, as Sydney had termed it, "the scenic route home."

"Dad says the ocean is never the same twice," Pete said, gesturing toward a small crowd of people who were standing near the rail and pointing out to sea. "I'll bet they've just spotted some dolphins, or a neat-looking ship or something. We've been coming here every summer since we were little kids, and we're still seeing new things. Right, Syd? Dad says we have to do everything we can to protect our oceans and all our waterways.''

Blake smiled indulgently. ''Your dad says a lot of good things. Tell me, guys, what's it like to have a United States senator for your father? Has he taken you with him when he campaigns?''

Pete only shrugged, but Paul cocked his head to one side as if seriously considering the question. ''What's it like? Gee, I guess I never really thought much about it. What does your father do, Blake?''

Blake reached up to scratch at the nape of his neck. ''My dad? He's a plumber, in Buffalo, specializing in heating and air-conditioning. Why do you ask?''

Paul grinned. ''A plumber, huh? Neat! Did he let you go out on jobs with him? Did you get to wear overalls and one of those plumber hats? What's it like to have a plumber for a father?''

Blake acknowledged that he had just been put in his place. ''Touché, Paul. I guess that answers my question. A father is a father. Right?''

''And a mother is a mother,'' Sydney put in, squeezing his arm. ''There are little differences, though, I have to admit. When I was little I rarely 'played house.' I wrote chapters. The boys spent some time playing Cowboys-and-Indians, but for the most part they borrowed Pops's ties and briefcase and went door-to-door to convince our neighbors to sign their petitions to end offshore dumping or some other project. I guess children will always imitate their parents, no matter what their parents do.''

"Which is why Mom gave up smoking for good when we were two and she caught Pete trying to put one of her cigarettes in his mouth. Right, Syd?''

"Right, kiddo. Hey, weren't you two guys planning on going bodysurfing this afternoon? I think you'd better get a move on if you don't want to miss the best waves.''

Uh-oh, Blake thought. *She's getting rid of the boys. Here it comes—time to pay the piper.*

"We've got time,'' Pete replied, unknowingly endearing himself to Blake. It wasn't as if Blake was afraid of Sydney. That was ridiculous. He was a grown man and could take care of himself. But then he had never felt like "prey'' before meeting Sydney. He just felt safer when the boys were around. Then Pete burst Blake's fragile bubble by adding, "But we'll leave if you two want to be alone.''

"That's not what I meant,'' Sydney protested, but then gave up as the boys nudged each other and Pete puckered his lips and made kissing motions to Paul. "Oh, I give up. You asked the boys what it's like to be the sons of a senator, Blake. You should have asked me what it's like to be the sister of twin monsters!''

"I think your nicknames for them say it all,'' Blake said, suddenly and quite unexpectedly happy with the boy's assessment of Sydney's wish to have Blake to herself. At least he hadn't been deluding himself that she was interested in him. It was nice to know he wasn't turning paranoid about the whole thing.

Besides, when he got right down to it, being pursued by the beautiful Sydney Blackmun didn't exactly come under the heading of cruel and unusual punishment. But that was all he was in the market for—just a friendly summer romance, no strings attached.

The twins ran ahead to buy a small bag of saltwater taffy while Sydney very obviously attempted to turn the subject away from the boys' teasing suggestions by pointing out a nearby bookstore jumbled in with the food stands and T-shirt shops that lined the land side of the boardwalk.

"There are lots of bookstores scattered along the boardwalk," she told him, "and more in town. Ocean City's really big on books. One of them even carries a wonderful selection of music. Do you like classical music, Blake? I didn't, until one of my teachers introduced me to it outside of the classroom. It's really beautiful, you know, if you don't have to understand it."

Blake decided to allow Sydney her diversion. "You may have a point there. I don't understand television ads for perfume or jeans."

"But you like them?"

He was beginning to relax, for he truly enjoyed Sydney's conversations. He never knew where they might lead. Blake lifted a hand to scratch behind his ear. "Actually, I think they're pretty lame. I don't believe anyone actually understands them. It's like *The Emperor's New Clothes*. Nobody wants to appear stupid by telling the king he's walking around in his long underwear. No, I just thought I'd mention it in order to sneak into this conversation while you took time for a breath.''

"Nut," Sydney responded, shaking her head. "You don't have to be nice. Do what everybody else does. Just say, 'Syd—shut up!' ''

"I'll remember that." Blake tried not to notice that she had somehow slipped her arm through his as they walked along. "I heard you playing some of Andrew Lloyd Webber's music this morning. Have you seen *Phantom of the Opera?*"

"Twice!" she answered, smiling up at him. "Once in London and then again on Broadway. I cried buckets both times. Now, don't tell me you didn't understand *Phantom,* because I won't believe you."

Blake assured her that he had understood the musical, but he refused to tell her that he had gone home after the show to bang away on his typewriter for the remainder of the night, attempting to plot his own happy ending for the doomed Phantom rather than working on the article he'd been paid to write for a small regional magazine.

He couldn't admit that to her. If he did, she would immediately assume he was some sort of starry-eyed romantic. She'd be right, as far as it went, but that didn't mean he was about to willingly hand her ammunition in her assault on his already crumbling intention to keep his distance. A light summer flirtation was one thing, but he wasn't interested in baring his soul to her, or to any woman. He'd done that once, and although the wounds might have healed, the scars were still tender.

If only she didn't smell so good.

He decided the time had come to move the discussion back to neutral ground. "Are there any second-hand bookstores on the island?"

"You love old books, too? I've been collecting books since I discovered Beatrix Potter. I think I was four at the time." She squeezed his arm and he deliberately moved away, telling her he was warm and wanted to take off his Windbreaker. Sydney waited patiently until he had slung the jacket over his shoulder and then took hold of his arm once more.

So much for diversionary tactics. Obviously he was up against a master. As he wasn't about to keep repeating his actions until he was walking along the boardwalk in nothing but his sneakers, and because he knew he enjoyed her touch, Blake gave up the fight. "Four? Isn't that a little young? Or are you telling me you were a child prodigy?"

Sydney laughed out loud, the sound delicious and infectious. "Blake! You make it sound like a curse. I couldn't help myself, honestly. When I was fourteen, and all arms and legs, I tried being dumb, just to see if the boys would be interested in a skinny, dumb brunette, but they weren't. It was Pops who told me never to be ashamed of my brain. Besides, according to Pops, my everyday conversation would never lead anyone to believe I had a brain larger than a mustard seed. He was right. Boys finally did notice me, but I don't think it was because of or in spite of my brain. I think I just plain grew up."

And in all the right places, Blake found himself thinking, and immediately squelched the thought. "So, you have a large collection of books."

Her eyes took on a soft, almost lover-like expression. "I adore everything about books. I love the feel of them, the smell of them. It's not enough to read them. When I find a book I like—and I do that a lot—I just have to own it. Thankfully my parents feel the same way, or they might have had me locked up years ago."

Blake pushed at the nosepiece of his glasses. His apartment in Manhattan was stacked with books he couldn't bear to give away. How many times had he lived on soup and peanut-butter sandwiches, just so he could add to his library?

"Many readers find writing a natural progression. Have you ever thought about following in your mother's footsteps?"

"Not me. Pops calls me a professional student. All I seem to do is go to school. This past year I tried English schools. They're great. And of course I start in Fairfield this fall. I can't seem to stay away from schools. But that's enough about me." Sydney's green eyes flashed mischievously. "Let's talk about you and your play. Tell me how you came to try your hand at— Oh, darn it." She pulled her arm free of his, and Blake didn't know whether to be relieved or disappointed. "Don't look now, Blake, but the terrible twosome is on its way back, bearing taffy. I hope they got me some of the cinnamon-flavored. It's so hot it burns your tongue. I love it."

They spoke in generalities now that the boys were with them again, with Pete and Paul doing most of the talking, which suited Blake, as Sydney had given him something to think about.

Sydney Blackmun was the most open, gregarious, fun-loving person he had ever met, bright, intelligent—but seemingly also a person totally without direction. It was as if she played at life, enjoying it to the hilt but never really becoming a part of it. Her stepfather called her a professional student, and Sydney appeared to have taken that as a compliment. Blake saw it as an accusation. To him, Sydney was all fluff—beautiful, enticing, intelligent fluff—but fluff just the same.

He obediently opened his mouth to let Sydney ply him with a piece of peppermint taffy she'd unwrapped for him. Her emerald eyes sparkled as she popped a piece of cinnamon taffy into her own mouth, then grinned up at him, telling him he was now truly a vacationer, having gotten his molars stuck together by the best taffy in town.

Unable to answer her, as he was fully occupied trying to chew the taffy, he pulled her close against his side as they continued their walk back to Delancey Place. She fit against him perfectly, as if those incredibly long, slim legs of hers had been expressly fashioned to match his own lengthy strides.

A man could get used to this sort of thing, this comfortably exciting feeling of freedom, yet belonging. He'd have to stop worrying about indulging in a summer romance with Sydney, stop believing she might be hurt when it was over. If Sydney played at life she probably had also been playing at Ocean City summer romances for years, and her pursuit of him could only be another game. He believed he finally understood the rules. Keep it light, keep it fun and enjoy it while it lasts. He could live with that.

Paul's question interrupted Blake's self-comforting thoughts. "Do you know why Egg Harbor is called Egg Harbor, Blake?"

Blake shook his head, trying to clear it for action. He looked down at Paul, who had been having a friendly argument with his brother about something. "What? No, I can't say as I do."

As they walked down the ramp leading from the boardwalk to Delancey Place, Paul willingly explained. "When the Dutch first landed in New Jersey around sixteen-oh-something they set out to explore all the bays and inlets, getting their bearings, I guess. Anyway, when they sailed into this one harbor there were so many eggs lying around—sea gull eggs, sandpiper eggs, all sorts of eggs—that they could barely see the sand on the beach. They named the place Eyren Haven, the harbor of eggs. From there it got changed to Little Egg Harbor, and then just plain Egg Harbor. Neat, huh?"

"Not half as neat as all the stories about the smugglers and pirates who used to hide in the bays and inlets," Pete said. "Eggs are one thing, but give me a good pirate story any day. The pine barrens around here used to be called Smuggler's Woods, because there were so many smugglers running around hiding their treasures there. When we're sixteen Dad says he's going to take us on a treasure hunt."

Sydney went up on tiptoe and leaned close to whisper in Blake's ear. "Personally, I think Pops is hoping they'll grow out of it by then. They can get their drivers' permits at sixteen, you know. But right now John Hancock is one of Pete's major idols, not because he signed the Declaration of Independence, but because good old John was one of the biggest smugglers going in those days."

"Were there pirates in New York, Blake?" Pete asked as they passed the condo and climbed the steps to Sydney's Folly.

Blake shot a look at his condo, knowing his typewriter was sitting up there on the desk, waiting for him, but he followed Sydney up the steps to her front porch, refusing to ask himself why he didn't just say goodbye and leave them on the pavement.

"Pirates? There are plenty of them there today, sport," he told Pete, winking at Sydney. "They wear pin-striped suits and hide out in a place called Wall Street." As Sydney laughed and the boys looked puzzled, Blake seriously considered the question. "I guess there were pirates and smugglers in New York. You know, I never really checked."

Paul shook his head. "That's poor. You have to know the history of your state. Dad says you can't be a really responsible citizen of your state, your country or even the world, if you don't pay attention to history. And know what? It's interesting." He turned to his sister. "Tell Blake about the history of this house."

"Only if you and Pete come inside and help me bring us all some lemonade. I made some fresh this morning."

As he appreciatively watched Sydney's long legs stride toward the front door, Blake, who had seated himself on the edge of the porch, mentally wrote off any notion that he was going to get any more work done today—and silently wondered if he was destined to go through the rest of the summer drinking lemonade that he didn't like.

Chapter Six

When Sydney came out of the house and sat down beside him, her bare legs dangling over the edge of the porch, he turned to her, only to have the breeze blow some of her long, black hair into his face. It smelled cleanly delicious and subtly lemon-scented. He sighed, reluctantly removing the strands with his hand. *Keep it light,* he reminded himself, his fingertips tingling after their contact with the silky softness.

"So, what do you want to know about the house?" Sydney asked, reaching into her pocket to pull out an elastic band which she used to secure her hair in a ponytail at her nape.

He found himself staring at the soft, vulnerable lines of her chin and throat, and wondered if her skin also tasted of lemons. What did he want to know about the house? The location of her bedroom would do for starters.

Keep it light, Blake, keep it light, he reminded himself yet again, gritting his teeth. You know the rules; she knows the rules. No harm, no foul.

"The house? Who cares? I want to know why the twins still look exactly alike but I now instantly know which is which as soon as one of them opens his mouth. I want to know why I'm sitting here, about to drink lemonade, when I should be upstairs, writing." He smiled at her, then sighed. "But I guess I'll settle for asking you about the history of the house. In two volumes or less, please."

Sydney primly clasped her hands in her lap, her legs crossed at the ankles as they lazily swung back and forth. "Okay. You want the abbreviated version. I guess I can do that. The house was built around the end of the nineteenth century, which stands to reason, as it is in the late-Victorian style, isn't it? Dozens of wealthy people from Philadelphia came here to build summer homes for their families, and I think mine was one of them.

"Would you believe this house used to be almost on the beach? It's true. But over the years the town has built the beach up and the house slowly moved backward—not actually, of course, but you know what I mean. Anyway, the house was built with a brick ground floor, no basement. The ground floor is used for storage and the real living was meant to take place on the upper three floors."

"Let me guess," Blake interrupted as Paul, already dressed in his bathing suit, came out of the house and handed him a glass of lemonade. "The house was built that way in order to take advantage of the ocean breezes."

"Right," Pete broke in, plopping down beside Blake, his slim body clad in a neon blue swimsuit. "The houses were even called 'upper cottages.' They were also built this way to keep the people who lived in them up above the mosquitos and flies. They don't fly all that high, you know." He frowned and shot a look at his sister. "The *bugs* don't fly that high—not the people."

"Don't forget the other reason," Paul said, dropping to his knees beside Sydney, so that the twins became a set of human bookends, pressing Blake and their sister even closer together. "The porches were built as high as the first floor in order to give the owner a better view of the ocean. Right, Syd?"

"Right again," she agreed, reaching over to ruffle his hair. "Now why don't you two head down to the beach. It has been nearly an hour since you had lunch. But leave the taffy."

Pete stood first, going over to pull his brother to his feet. "Come on, bro. Can't say we can't take a hint. They want to be *alone*."

Sydney closed her eyes and shook her head. "My brothers. I think I'll keep them—under lock and key!" She turned to Blake. "Now, where were we? Oh, yes. The abbreviated version. There's really not much more to add."

"I'll bet," Blake slid in, looking around to watch the boys leave. They seemed rather used to being dismissed by their sister so she could be alone with her latest boyfriend. The thought only solidified his conclusions about her. Not that he believed Sydney to be promiscuous—he would never believe that. But he couldn't help wondering if she kept score, measuring this year's Ocean City romance against those of other summers.

"No, really," Sydney told him, tugging at his sleeve. "There isn't much more to tell, so turn around and pay attention, if you please. The original owners only lived in the house for a few years, and for the rest of the time it has been a rooming house. It was vacant when I found it, and I decided to spend the summer turning it into a bed-and-breakfast, before school starts again in the fall. It's great fun. There. Have I said enough? Too much? Would you like the cook's tour?"

She was already scrambling to her feet, leaving Blake little option but to follow her.

They entered through the front door, which he already knew led directly to a center hall that twisted and turned toward the back of the house, with rooms leading off it at odd angles. Sydney had unwrapped another piece of saltwater taffy, offering him some first, which he declined.

"Um, another cinnamon!" she said, sinking her teeth into the taffy at one end, then pulling on the rest of it so that it stretched out thinly before she doubled it over and popped all of it in her mouth.

The action reminded Blake of the way he'd played with bubble gum as a boy, but when Sydney did it the action lost a lot of its innocence.

This bothered him. But what bothered him more was the dawning realization that Sydney was completely aware that she was slowly driving him out of his mind.

"What's this room going to be?" he asked quickly, averting his eyes from her moist mouth.

"I'm not sure yet," she said, standing just inside the doorway. "I plan this floor to be the common area— except for the office, of course. I already know the back room, the one with all the windows, will be the solarium, but this room could either be the library or the living room."

Blake poked his head into the room, seeing the built-in bookshelves that had been stripped down to the bare wood. "Does the other room have book-shelves as well?"

Sydney nodded. "I only wish there were more. Mom says if I don't soon get my book collection out of her house she's going to begin charging me rent. Now the guests will be able to read my books. Works out well, don't you think?"

She brushed past Blake to skip down the hall to an-other room. "This is going to be the billiard room. Can't you just see it? Cues lining the walls, a big Tif-fany light over a gigantic pool table that has a deep burgundy felt cover and old-fashioned fringed pock-ets." She rubbed her palms together. "I can't wait!"

"You play pool?" Blake asked, not surprised that *he* wasn't surprised when she nodded her head in the affirmative.

"Pops said that if I had been pushed to it I could have financed my entire college education playing eight-ball. I guess I am a bit of a shark. Do you play?"

"A little," Blake answered, remembering that he had—after losing his scholarship—eaten more than one meal thanks to his skill with a cue. He backed out of the room and continued down the hall. "I've already seen the kitchen, if you remember. It's going to be a bed-and-*breakfast*. Who will be doing the cooking?" He wouldn't have turned a hair if she had told him she was a *cordon bleu* chef, having spent a year being a "professional student" in France—except that he had already heard differently from the twins.

"A cook, of course. The place is going to be open year-round, and I'll be in school." Sydney's pert nose wrinkled delightfully. "Besides, I don't think it's safe to let me close to a stove on a daily basis."

Blake rounded the corner of the hallway that he knew would lead him to the street side of the house and the turret he had already noticed from the sidewalk. He took three steps and then stopped, amazed at the sight that greeted him.

He had supposed the turret would contain a small area to be used for a sitting room or some such purpose. What he saw was that the turret had been fashioned to hold the massive wooden staircase that curved upward to the second floor. Painted white, with a dark mahogany railing topping the balusters, the staircase hugged the outside wall as it rose gracefully, to end in a small arched balcony that overlooked the first floor.

"Damn," Blake said quietly, impressed.

Sydney came up behind him to place a hand on his waist. "Kind of takes your breath away, doesn't it? I was almost ready to give up on the idea of buying this house when my parents got done pointing out all the pitfalls. But once I saw this staircase, I knew I had to have it. Oh, they can try recreating stuff like this, but nothing beats the original. All these years, and the treads don't even creak when the twins jump up and down on them. That's craftsmanship! Hey—stay here a minute. I've been dying to try this out ever since I moved in."

Without waiting for his answer, Sydney ran to a nearby vase, plucked out a wilting daisy, then scampered up the stairs, to stand at the edge of the balcony, her palms pressed against the banister. Looking toward the first floor without really looking at Blake, she sniffed at the flower, then rested her cheek against her hand, sighed deeply and intoned sorrowfully, "'O Romeo, Romeo! wherefore art thou Romeo?'"

She had to be kidding! Did she really think he was about to reenact the balcony scene from *Romeo and Juliet* with her? "Tough luck, Julie. Romeo went out for pizza," Blake answered swiftly, laughing at her comical expression of emotional distress.

Without abandoning her tragic posture, Sydney slid her gaze to meet Blake's. "'Deny thy father, and refuse thy name;'" she continued through gritted teeth, "'Or, if thou wilt not, be but sworn my love,/And I'll no longer be a Capulet.'"

Obviously she wasn't about to give it up.

She wanted a romantic love scene, did she? Well, two could play this game. He took hold of the railing and slowly began his ascent to the balcony. "'I take thee at thy word,'" he intoned deeply, one hand to his chest. "'Call me but love, and I'll be new baptized:/Henceforth I never will be Romeo.'"

As he moved up the stairs, Sydney turned to him to recite, "'What man art thou that thus bescreened in night/So stumblest on my counsel?'"

Blake reached the balcony, to stand a breath away from Sydney, his hand joining hers as she held the daisy. "'What's in a name?'" he asked huskily, his fingers stroking the back of her hand, "'that which we call a rose/By any other name would smell as sweet.'"

Sydney's cheeks flushed a becoming pink as she looked up into his face. She spoke out of the corner of her mouth, her voice not nearly so assured as it had been. "Um...that's not the right line, Blake. You made me lose my place. Wait—don't move! I'll fake the rest and cut to the chase."

Discarding the flower over the edge of the railing, Blake put his hands on her waist, pulling her close against his body, his head descending so that their lips were only scant inches apart. "Wrong, Juliet. *I'll* cut to the chase."

The next thing he knew he was standing alone on the balcony and Sydney was running lightly down the stairs to the floor below. He leaned over the railing, watching as she picked up the flower, raising it to him as if in salute. "Bravo! *Bravissimo!*" she called brightly. Too brightly.

Fluff. Summer romance. Keep it light. Blake remembered these words as he berated himself for moving too fast, too soon, and for breaking his own rules. Maybe he didn't know all the rules after all—at least not those on Sydney's list. He continued to look at her closely as he descended the staircase, searching her expression to see if he had frightened her.

"You were wonderful," she continued, replacing the flower in its vase, "even if it was the edited version. But what else should I have expected for a writer of short stories. Don't tell anybody, but there are times I believe Shakespeare could have used a good editor. Anyway, thank you for fulfilling my fantasy."

She seemed to have recovered her usual good humor, if indeed she had ever lost it.

"And that's your only fantasy?" he asked, leaning against the banister at the bottom of the staircase.

Sydney shrugged. "Hey, I became an English Literature freak while in London. What else would you expect?"

Blake turned back to face her, still aching for the kiss they hadn't shared. He felt as if he had just tried catching a will-o'-the-wisp, using a net with an unexplained hole in it. "From you? Anything."

She didn't appear to take offense at his words, but only turned and headed past him, back up the staircase, yet Blake could feel the new tension between them. "Come on, I'll finish showing you the house."

He wanted to protest; he wanted to grab onto her arm, pull her close and finish what she had started; he wanted to talk to her, demand she explain the rules for her game. But he also knew his safest bet was simply to follow her lead.

A quick tour of the second floor was accomplished in a few minutes, as all the bedrooms were vacant and very much alike, and Sydney rapidly passed by the closed door to her own room, heading for the much more mundane staircase leading up to the third floor.

"There are two staircases to this floor, one in front and these old servant stairs. This floor has about the same layout as the second, only smaller, not covering the same area as the other floors, so I won't make you tour it, but I wanted you to see the roof," Sydney told him as she opened the door to the rear of the house. "Here we go—what do you think?"

Blake came to a halt just outside the door on the flat roof, which sat above approximately one third of the second story of the house. He looked around, seeing no more than an expanse of nothingness. "Yep," he said shortly, for he hadn't been able to do much more than mumble monosyllables in between Sydney's animated descriptions of what she planned to do with the rooms. "It's a roof, all right."

Sydney shook her head vehemently. "No, no! You have no imagination." She skipped to the center of the roof and began pointing out her plans for the area while his muscles bunched, ready to rescue her if she strayed too close to the edge. "Here, right where I'm standing, is where the five-person hot tub is going to be."

"The hot tub?" he repeated blankly.

"Yes. The sauna will be on your right, smack up against the house wall, and there will be a trellis starting at the wall on your left, next to the drinks and soda bar. It'll go up about fifteen feet—the trellis, that is—then come out this way, sort of like a roof, until it ends on the other side of the hot tub and the raised observation deck, where people can sit and watch the tide roll in."

Blake shook his head. "The five-person hot tub *and* a sauna. I should have known."

He was not surprised when she ignored his comment. "The sitting and sunning area won't have any covering, but I think I'll have Grecian pillars scattered here, there and everywhere, just to make it feel private. And plants, lots of plants, and ivy growing on the trellis. I like flowering plants like wisteria, but even though the vines would be pretty, they might draw bees, and I wouldn't want any of my guests to get stung." She stood back, her hands on her hips, and wrinkled her nose. "Well, what do you think? Is it too much?"

"Too much?" Blake repeated, nearly choking. He had been wrong. She wasn't a will-o'-the-wisp. She was a roller coaster—a double-loop state-of-the-art roller coaster—and he might just as well sit back and enjoy the ride until it was over!

He wrinkled his own nose and shook his head. "Naw, Syd, it's not too much. For the rest of the world maybe, but not for you. For you, it's just about right."

And so saying, he took off his glasses, sat down on the roof and laughed until his sides hurt.

"Hi, Mom! This is a surprise. How's Paris?" Sydney laid down her brush, kicked the door of the freestanding red telephone booth shut with one sneakered foot and sat down on the small bench inside it, silently hoping the paint was finally completely dry. "What? The twins? Oh, they're down on the beach with our neighbor, Blake Mansfield. It's high tide."

Sydney listened for a moment, then hastened into speech. "Relax, Mom, Blake's a very nice man. Honestly. No, he did not 'pick me up.' As a matter of fact, I think I picked him up. Seriously, Mom, Blake is my new neighbor. He rented the second-floor condo next door to my place. He's here for the whole summer. He's young, terribly handsome, and a writer. Now, you know if he's a writer he can't be all that bad. What? Yes, Mother, I know the Marquis de Sade kept his memoirs. What has that got to do with anything?"

Sydney pressed a hand to her mouth to stifle a giggle and listened while her mother read her a small lecture on the foolhardiness of trusting every stranger she met. As her mother spoke, Sydney looked out through one of the leaded-glass panes of the telephone booth to the nearby staircase where she and Blake had just two hours earlier enacted their short, strangely intense rendition of the *Romeo and Juliet* balcony scene.

Her mother's voice coming through the telephone line brought Sydney back to attention. "Pardon me? Oh, yes, the twins are fine, Mom. They won a prize in the kite-flying contest. A couple of local girls beat them out for the grand prize, though. For a while there I thought Pete was going to smack young Mary Ellen McGinley in the chops. He'll probably grow up to marry her.... Yes, Mom, I've been good. I'm so busy fixing up Sydney's Folly, I haven't had time to be bad. Is Pops around? I'd like to talk to him when you're done telling me all about Paris."

Ten minutes later Adam Richardson's voice came to her over the wire, his jovial greeting bringing a smile to Sydney's lips. "Hi, Pops. Are you keeping her in line? I mean, she didn't take one look at the Bastille and rush back to the hotel room to start jotting down notes for her next book, did she? That's terrific. Keep it that way. She needs a real vacation. Listen, Pops, can you keep a straight face? I mean, with Mom in the room and all? Otherwise, she'll probably panic and be back here on the next plane, all set to go into her overprotective mothering mode like she did when I was thirteen. You'll get rid of her? Nothing final, I hope. Good. I knew I could count on you."

She listened while Adam asked his wife to get his drink from the bedroom of their hotel suite, then paused a moment, gathering her courage. "Pops, do you think I'm flighty? Well, not precisely flighty. Do you think I take on too many projects? No, I'm not talking about Sydney's Folly, I already know you understand why I bought the place. But, Pops, I've met this man since moving in here. His name is Blake Mansfield. He's renting the condo next door. He's a writer, and he came to Ocean City for the summer to try turning one of his short stories into a play and—"

Sydney hesitated, not really knowing what to say, or how to say it. "He seems sort of sad, as if there's something about his life that keeps him from being really happy, even when he tries. Not that he isn't a lot of fun, because he is, really. But he looks so vulnerable. Yes, that's the word. Vulnerable. And devastatingly handsome," she added quietly, hoping her stepfather hadn't heard her.

She held the receiver, nodding silently while Adam Richardson gave her a typically fatherly warning about "vulnerable"-looking men.

"The twins like him too, Pops," she interrupted at last, knowing it wasn't much of an endorsement. "And it's not as if I've met the love of my life or anything—I just think he's nice, that's all. And I want to help him. But I don't want to be pushy. You're a man, Pops, so you might know how Blake would feel about this idea I've had. I just thought, maybe if I called Uncle Willie, he'd—"

Sydney listened quietly again, sighing resignedly. "Yes, Pops," she said at last, laughing. "I do remember the puppy I brought home that summer. Yes, I also remember the fleas. But we've all learned to love Pundit, haven't we?"

She replaced the receiver a few minutes later and leaned back against the leaded-glass panes of the booth to consider the advice Adam had given her. "You've always had good instincts about people, Syd," he had said. "You liked me right away, didn't you? Just be careful, sweetheart. Vulnerable *and* devastatingly handsome is a potent combination."

Sydney rose and went to retrieve her brush, planning to finish applying the second coat of paint to the outside of the booth. "All right, Blake," she whispered quietly, chancing a look up at the balcony, her stomach doing a small flip. "Now that I have the go-ahead from Pops—sort of—it's every man for himself. I'm going to follow my instincts and see where they lead. And if they lead to you, my friend, well, you just aren't going to know what's hit you!"

Chapter Seven

"Sydney! Darling child! Can that possibly be you? You look so dark. Positively exotic. It becomes you. Now, come here and give an old man a kiss."

Sydney was already halfway down the porch steps, her arms outflung as she raced toward the silver-haired man standing at the edge of the walkway. "Uncle Willie! I don't believe it! I was going to call you later today. What are you doing here? You never leave New York."

She threw herself into the man's arms and gave him resounding kisses on both cheeks, then stood back to admire his natty gray suit. "How utterly New York you look, Uncle Willie." She reached up to loosen the neat Windsor knot on his mauve silk tie. "But this is New Jersey in the summertime. No ties, no starch, and most definitely no Italian suits!" She stopped her assault on the designer tie and gave him another hug. "Oh, I'm so glad to see you!"

Wilbur Langley, publisher of Langley Books, which included publishing all of Courtney Blackmun's best-sellers, gently disentangled his dapper self from Sydney's enthusiastic embrace and held her at arm's length. "Those legs of yours go all the way to your neck, don't they?" he commented, shaking his head. "Ah, darling, if you weren't Courtney's little girl—and if she wouldn't have my head on a platter if I so much as thought it—I'd ask you to marry me."

"Marry you, Uncle Willie?" Sydney repeated, arching one expressive eyebrow. "And I thought you always said that three marriages were more than enough for any man." She slipped an arm through his and began pulling him toward the house. "So, what do you think of the place so far? Isn't it just fantastic? Isn't it everything I told you it was?"

Wilbur looked up at the house. It had come a long way since Sydney had bought it, but still had a long way to go before it resembled anything near her glowing description of her "project in progress." Stopping on the top step of the porch he turned to look at Sydney. "Do you want the truth or a pretty lie? I'm amenable either way."

Sydney wrinkled her nose. "Oh, pooh, Uncle Willie. Use your imagination. So, are you going to be my first paying customer, like you promised?"

"I don't know. How much would it cost me to be allowed to stay away?"

"That wasn't nice," Sydney pointed out, giving him another kiss.

By now they were inside, where the smell of fresh paint and varnish was nearly overpowering. Wilbur pulled out a snow-white handkerchief and pressed it to his nose. "That promise was for late August, if I remember correctly, darling, so I'm safe until then, I suppose. I'm only here today to check up on you. Courtney smells a rat."

"You're kidding! I haven't done anything, honestly I haven't." Sydney let out a great sigh as Wilbur's left eyebrow rose a fraction. "I give up. I should have known it would take an SOS from Mom to get you down here. How does she do it? I tell you, Uncle Willie, I don't think I'll ever get anything past that woman."

"Not while you're so transparent, you won't. You shouldn't have had Adam send your mother out of the room while you spoke to him, you know. Courtney has a mind for plots and is not easily deceived. She was on the telephone to me late last night, begging me to come down here and see what you're up to this time."

Sydney collapsed against the kitchen counter. "You know something, Uncle Willie? When I was young, I always tried to make excuses to run my fingers through Mom's hair."

The publisher looked askance at her. "You know how much I dislike playing the straight man to your jokes, darling. But I shall ask anyway—what were you looking for in Courtney's hair?"

Sydney grinned. "Why, I thought it would be obvious. I was looking for the extra set of eyes she must have had on the back of her head! How else could she always know what mischief I was up to? Not that I am—up to something, that is. Anyway, what has her fertile mind thought up this time?"

"She thinks it's a man. A neighbor, I believe. But of course I told her that was impossible. You're just a baby, I said. Now, looking at you, I realize why your mother laughed at me. I also realize at last how old I am," he added softly, pulling a face. "It makes me wonder what dearest Clarissa sees in me."

"Clarissa? So that's this season's name," Sydney said cheerfully, pulling Wilbur out onto the side porch and directing him to one of the wicker chairs. "Nice name, Clarissa. How old is she, Uncle Willie—twelve?"

Wilbur didn't take offense, as his long string of youthful lady loves was almost as legendary as his prowess in picking best-selling authors. "How you wound me. Clarissa has cut all her second teeth, my dear, being all of twenty-eight. Positively ancient, now that I think of it. She's on Broadway, or doing cabaret work, or something. Now, are you going to tell me about this mysterious man in your life, or is your poor mother going to be forced to come storming back home?"

Sydney put Wilbur off while she went into the kitchen to fetch them some lemonade, and then delayed her answer a while longer as she gave him a detailed description of the twins' kite and their plans to carry off first prize in the sand-sculpting contest. She had just launched into a recital of her culinary successes when Wilbur silenced her by raising one manicured hand.

"His name, darling, or I shall phone Courtney," he warned, his tone as smoothly silky as his designer tie, and just as intimidating. Wilbur had been her friend for as long as she could remember, but Sydney had never underestimated his intelligence, or his ability to cut to the bottom line.

She collapsed against the back of the wicker chair, her chin on her chest. "His name is Blake Mansfield, and he's a writer who is living in the condo next door for the summer." She sat forward and turned to glare into the publisher's eyes. "He's the reason I was going to phone you today. I wanted you to take a look at his work. And if you're mean to him, Uncle Willie, I swear I'll make your life a living hell!"

Wilbur dismissed her threat with a wave of his hand. "Mansfield. Mansfield. No, never heard of him. What does he write?"

"Short stories," Sydney answered, brightening, for Wilbur hadn't dismissed her request out of hand. "He's down here to expand one of them into a play. Uncle Willie, don't you think you could possibly take a—"

He cut her off. "No, I don't think I could. I don't even think I want to, darling. Your mother was my last discovery, my swan song as it were. I'm old now—though not *too* old—but content to rest on my laurels and let everyone else do the real work. And may I point out my expertise is novels, not plays? I backed one once and lost an unconscionable amount of money. Besides, what if I hate his work?"

Sydney was out of her chair, pacing the wooden deck. "But you couldn't hate it. Blake is terribly gifted."

"You've read his work?"

Sydney bowed her head. She knew he'd ask that question sooner or later, only she had hoped it would be later. "No, not really. But Blake is extremely intelligent, and very articulate. He has a great sense of humor. And he says his short story was successful. It may even have been reprinted in an anthology or something. Surely it wouldn't hurt to take a teensy peek at some of his work? Come on, Uncle Willie. Be a sport!"

"Don't whine, Sydney, it's not like you. I'm going back to New York tonight," Wilbur said, consulting his watch as he stood up. "Bring the boy to dinner—there must be a decent place to eat somewhere on this island—after all, I do have to see him before I can report to Courtney, don't I? But no talk of plays, understand? For now, I'm going back to your parents' condo and lie down. They gave me the key before they left, knowing that you and those terrible boys had decided to camp out here like vagabonds. Clarissa, bless her, is already sunning her sweet self on the deck."

He ignored Sydney's pout to add a further condition. "And keep those brothers of yours at the opposite end of the table from me, thank you. The last time I was foolish enough to dine with them in public, one of the nasty little monsters threw up on my shoe."

Sydney laughed at the memory of that fateful dinner at The Plaza. "That was Paul, and he was only five years old. We didn't know it, but both of them were coming down with chicken pox. Surely you can't hold that against them, Uncle Willie?''

"I can if I want to, darling,'' he said as the chauffeur held open the door to the long silver limousine. "I'm old now, and there's no end of things I find I can get away with by pleading galloping senility. And one other thing, my dear. Drop the words 'Uncle Willie' from your vocabulary, if you please. I've allowed you, and only you, to call me by that ridiculous name, but now I think I must withdraw my permission. Clarissa will be joining us for dinner, you understand. The dear child has this tendency to giggle, and I know you wouldn't wish to set her off.''

"You're uncharacteristically quiet, Sydney,'' Blake said as they walked along together, the twins having run ahead and disappeared from sight into the crowd of vacationers strolling the boardwalk after they had all said their goodbyes to Wilbur outside the restaurant. "Didn't you enjoy yourself tonight? I thought Wilbur was great. Thanks for inviting me along to dinner. The man certainly has a wide range of interests. I couldn't believe he knew so much about basketball.''

Sydney looked up at him, her emerald eyes cloudy. "Wilbur knows a lot about almost everything.'' She stopped walking and asked, "Blake, why didn't you tell me you played basketball?''

Blake stopped as well, pulling her over to the rail and out of the way of the milling crowd. "I guess the subject never came up. Should it have?'' he questioned, somehow disliking her tone. She didn't sound angry. She sounded hurt, as if he had been keeping a secret from her, which was ridiculous.

His past wasn't a secret. It was just something he didn't particularly like talking about. "All right," he went on, trying to wipe the disappointed look from her face. "It's late for this, but I'll admit it. I played basketball in grade school, in high school, in college. It's a dirty job, I know, but somebody had to do it."

Her jaw jutted forward defiantly. Great. He had gotten her over her hurt, all right. Now she was angry! "That's not funny, Blake. That's not funny in the least."

Blake exhaled wearily. "So I'm not a born comic. Look, Syd—"

"Oh, I'm sorry," she interrupted, placing a hand on his arm, so that he felt his momentary anger drain away. "I don't mean to argue. But you played at forward for one of the best college teams in America for three years, and I saw the look on your face when Wilbur finally put two and two together and began rattling off your college statistics like some television sports announcer. Those memories hurt you. I didn't expect to know your life story—it's just that you could at least have warned me. If I had known about the basketball, about the way you feel about it, I would have warned Wilbur off before we met you for dinner."

Blake felt his jaw muscles tighten. "Do I seem that helpless? Well, I'm not. I'm a big boy, Sydney, not one of the twins. I don't need anybody to protect me."

"And I'm not trying to be your mother. I'm your *friend!*" she exploded, giving him a sharp poke in the midsection with her index finger, as if for emphasis. Then, just as quickly, the fire went out of her eyes. She turned to the railing, looking out toward the incoming tide as she spoke. "Wilbur said the pros were after you until the injury happened," she mumbled softly, as if reluctant to bring up the subject again. "You must have been devastated when you had to give up basketball. It's terrible to lose a dream."

Blake looked down on Sydney's bowed head, longing to take her in his arms. He hadn't expected this from Sydney, from his will-o'-the-wisp. She was hurting for him, somehow instinctively knowing that being forced to give up basketball had been the most difficult thing he'd done in his life. "It's not *that* terrible, Sydney. I survived."

"And now?" she asked, looking up at him, the breeze coming off the ocean tangling her long black hair around her throat and cheeks.

"And now I'm wondering if you're ready for a second dessert," he answered, reaching out to push one errant silky lock behind her ear. "You hardly touched the chocolate mousse at the restaurant."

Sydney laughed weakly. "Now who's acting like a mother? Don't try changing the subject with me the way you did at dinner with Wilbur. He's a gentleman and took the hint, but I'm no gentleman. What was it like when the surgeon told you your knee would keep you from ever playing again?"

His forearms resting on the metal rails, Blake looked out over the dark ocean for a long time before answering, watching as the moon caught at the whitecaps heading for the shore.

"It wasn't like Christmas morning after Santa had been there, that's for sure," he said at last, taking her by the elbow and steering her back into the flow of people. "My whole world had been basketball, ever since the sixth grade. I'd had one surgery while I was still in high school, but the last injury, in the play-offs near the end of my junior year of college, was the worst. I was in a cast for eight weeks, so I had plenty of time to build up a real head of self-pity when the final word came down from the doctors."

"At least you still had your scholarship," Sydney said. Wilbur had mentioned that Blake had gone to school on "a full ride," which meant his entire tuition and other expenses had been paid for by the college.

Blake laughed, and the laughter sounded bitter, even to his own ears. "I gave it up, Syd. Oh, the school wanted me to keep it, but I told them I got the scholarship because I could play ball. If I couldn't play ball any more, the scholarship was nothing but pity money."

He laughed again, shaking his head. "Damn, but I was an arrogant bastard. I never told my parents I gave up the scholarship, and I nearly had to quit school halfway through my senior year. As it was, I worked three part-time jobs just to keep myself in peanut butter and jelly." He smiled down at her. "And I played a little pool."

"But you hung in there and got your degree."

Blake nodded. "And that, my *friend,* and a buck will get you a cup of coffee—at least when you want to write, that is. I majored in American Literature and always planned to write—someday—when I retired from the pros. Someday just came sooner than I expected, and me without any memoirs of my glory days to peddle to publishers like Wilbur.''

They turned down the ramp and exited the boardwalk onto Delancey Place. Sydney took Blake's hand as they made their way through the darkness. ''That's another thing,'' she said, squeezing his fingers, ''not that I want to argue again. I could have cheerfully murdered you for not allowing Wilbur to read your play. You wouldn't have been imposing on him. He likes you. He *asked* to see it—after telling *me* he'd do no such thing.''

That stopped him, and he had the sudden feeling that Sydney seemed to see him as some sort of work in progress, like her bed-and-breakfast. Did she take on a project every summer, along with a summer love?

''You asked him to read my play? Sydney, you had no right to do that. What are you doing—working toward some scouting badge I don't know about? If I didn't look for a handout when I hurt my knee, I'm sure not looking for one now!'' He began pulling her along the sidewalk. ''Come on. It's time all do-gooders were home in bed.''

She had no choice but to walk with him, but he soon discovered that it didn't mean she felt there was nothing more to say. ''I wasn't trying to offer you a handout, Blake, and neither was Wilbur,'' she said, rapidly becoming breathless as his long strides caused her to have to nearly run to keep up with him.

''Honestly, I can't think of another person who would be so stubbornly bullheaded as to turn down a chance to have his writing critiqued by Wilbur Langley, one of the most respected editors to ever come out of New York. I mean, if *I* were going to write a book I know I'd go down on my hands and knees if Wilbur Langley were to—*oh!*''

Blake abruptly halted just outside his condo and brought Sydney up against his chest by the simple action of tugging on her hand.

For a woman he believed to be intent on a lighthearted summer romance she certainly knew how to get to him. And as a man who told himself he was intent on concentrating on his career and keeping clear of roller-coaster rides, he certainly was letting her get to him. "Syd," he groaned, searching through the darkness to see her face, her bright, beautiful, caring face, "shut up!"

And with that he pulled her completely into his arms, his mouth coming down to claim hers in a kiss that had been born equally of frustration and desire.

Chapter Eight

Sydney sat in the middle of the kitchen floor as the morning sunshine came through the uncurtained windows, a half dozen wilted daisy petals decorating her bare knees. She held a partially empty vase of fading flowers in front of her and stared at it.

"I'm going to keep doing this until it comes out right, so you guys had better get with the program," she warned the daisies before pulling out another bloom. "He loves me, he loves me not," she gritted through clenched teeth, tugging off two petals. "He loves me, he loves me not, he loves me—"

"Hey, Paul, get in here, you've got to see this. Syd's sitting in the middle of the floor, killing flowers."

Sydney scrambled to her feet, carrying the vase over to the sink. "I was going to throw them out this morning, anyway, smarty-pants," she said, returning to bend down and pick up the mess she'd made. "You want some breakfast?"

Paul stuck his head around the corner, his dark hair still tousled from sleep. "Is our government still a two-party system? Of course we want breakfast. We're so hungry we'll even eat what you make for us, right, Pete?" He came completely into the kitchen. "You killing those flowers over Blake, sis? We thought you took a long time coming home last night. Did he kiss you?"

Sydney shot him a look that threatened imminent mayhem, then turned to open the cabinet beside the sink. "Let's see. I've got instant oatmeal—your personal favorite, Paul—or I could make you both some scrambled eggs on toast. Did I mention that I'm going to begin using imitation eggs now? That cholesterol thing, you know. You're never too young to watch your cholesterol intake."

Pete shoved his brother as Paul walked past him. "You and your big mouth. Oatmeal or pretend eggs. Why don't you tease her some more, huh? See if you can score a few more points off her? Maybe we'll get real lucky and she'll make us some stewed prunes."

Paul hung his head and walked over to briefly touch Sydney on the shoulder. "Sorry, Syd. I didn't mean to embarrass you or anything. Besides," he said, brightening, "Pete started it."

"At least I didn't ask if Blake kissed her, for criminey's sake," Pete put in, sliding his long legs beneath the kitchen table. "But now that Paul brought it up... did he? Kiss you, I mean."

Sydney turned to face her brothers, who were looking at her as if they were recognizing for the first time that she was a female. Yes, Blake had kissed her. Twice, as a matter of fact. And both kisses had been absolutely glorious. Then he had walked her to her door—which was a good thing, for her knees had somehow turned to gelatin—before turning away without saying a single word. Not that it was any of Pete or Paul's business.

"What would it take to have you withdraw that question, Pete?" she asked, holding out the box of instant oatmeal, the one with the overpowering imitation apple-and-cinnamon flavoring.

"You're offering us a bribe?" Paul questioned, his brows lowered so that, just for a moment, he looked very much like his father.

"Bribery?" Sydney grinned. "That's such a nasty word. I prefer to call it an amicable alternative to chemically engineered eggs."

The twins exchanged glances, then answered together, "Pancakes. And bacon."

"You got 'em," Sydney answered quickly, returning the oatmeal box to the cabinet and heading for the refrigerator to take out the pancake batter she had made last night at midnight because she had been unable to sleep after leaving Blake and his impassioned kisses at the front door of Sydney's Folly. "I'm happy to see that you're both reasonable men. Now, what are you two planning for this morning? I've got to finish the trim in the solarium. There must be a dozen or more windows in that room. Any chance I can get either of you to lend me a hand?"

She could almost hear the gears turning in their heads as they fought for an excuse to what Pete had already jokingly termed Sydney's Slave Labor Summer Camp.

"We're going over to Blake's to see if we can get him to play a little B-ball down at the recreation center," Paul said as he opened a nearby cabinet to get out three plates. "Uncle Wilbur says he was one of the best. We figure maybe he can give us a couple of pointers."

Sydney felt her heart skip a beat. "Boys," she said, slitting open a new package of bacon, "maybe that's not such a good idea. I mean, Blake was injured pretty badly during his junior year of college—so much so that he had to give up the game. I know it has been a half dozen or more years since then, but I wouldn't want to see him trying to play just to please you guys."

"His knee is okay, Syd," Pete argued. "It just isn't good enough for the pros, that's all. Uncle Wilbur explained it to us, don't you remember?" He shook his head. "Poor Blake. It's got to be awful, being so tall and not being able to play basketball. I mean, now he's only tall, right?"

"Oh good," Sydney sniped, shaking her head. "Why don't you just go running over to Blake's and share that little thought with him? You'll probably cheer him up so much he'll jump into the ocean the first chance he gets!"

Pete threw up his hands protectively. "Whoa, sis, don't attack. I didn't mean anything, honest. I was just thinking out loud."

"So that's where you went wrong," Paul put in, laying a handful of silverware on the table. "You were thinking again, Pete. Mustn't do that. It's dangerous. Why, you might even hurt something."

Sydney poured out four perfect circles of batter and waited until bubbles formed on the top of each pancake before quickly flipping them over—all of them making the transition in one piece. She wasn't exactly an expert yet, but she was getting the hang of this cooking business. "All right, Paul, knock it off. I know what Pete meant. And I guess it wouldn't hurt to ask Blake to play some basketball with you. I'm just being overprotective—like Mom."

She wrinkled up her nose and pressed her hands to her throat in mock dismay. Well, not quite mock dismay. Blake had accused her of trying to mother him. "There's a depressing thought! Do you think I'm in danger of becoming motherly?"

The twins laughed out loud at this lunacy and breakfast time passed without further discussion of Blake, something that made Sydney extremely happy, or at least she told herself it did. At least it gave her time to think of a way to make Blake think of her as other than meddlesome, or motherly.

"Pivot left, Pete—toward the basket!" Blake yelled before releasing the ball in a shotgun pass toward the spot the twin should be occupying in the next millisecond. Pete turned, caught the ball, set himself, and put it cleanly through the hoop. "All right! See how that works?"

Blake trotted over to the boys and they exchanged high-fives. "Your turn, Paul," he said, walking back to mid-court, wiping his forehead with the bottom of his stretched-out, sweaty T-shirt. "Pete, you guard me now. I'll try a quick pass to Paul and he'll follow up with a baseline shot."

"Wouldn't it be easier with two equally matched teams?"

Blake turned to see Sydney standing at the edge of the court, her long black hair pulled back in a no-nonsense ponytail. She looked tall and cool and totally incapable of lifting a basketball through a hoop ten feet off the ground.

He pushed at the nosepiece of his glasses, even though they remained tightly in place, thanks to the band that held them to his head. It was an unconscious gesture, one he usually resorted to when either confused or, during his teenage years, when he was nervous about something.

He turned to the boys. "All right. Who wants her?"

The three had been on the outdoor court for well over an hour, either practicing plays or joining in quick pickup games with anyone who came along. But now there were just the three of them again, and Blake was in the mood for a little two-on-two. His knee didn't hurt. As a matter of fact, he felt great.

And Sydney's arrival at the court, for some unknown reason, made him feel even greater. He might even show off for her a little bit.

He pushed at his nosepiece again, hiding a smile as Sydney deftly snatched the ball from Pete and spun it perfectly on top of her right index finger. Hadn't he learned anything yet? If Sydney played basketball as well as she kissed, he might be in for his best contest of the morning.

"I'll take her," Paul piped up as his brother jabbed him in the ribs. "But we play two games to twenty-one, and next game I get Blake."

"Fair enough," Sydney said, walking to center court as she extracted a pink neon terry-cloth head-band from her pocket and pulled it over her fore-head. "A half-court game, of course, Blake? You wouldn't want to take advantage of the fact that I'm a female."

"Of course not," he answered, marveling at her long legs, which rose gracefully from the high-top sneakers she was wearing. Did she really think it necessary to remind him she was a woman? "And Pete and I will even spot you five points."

Sydney's smile was positively evil. "You're on, buster!" She picked up the ball and tossed it to Pete as she stared at Blake. "Paul, you've got your brother. This bozo's mine!"

There were several words Blake could have applied to Sydney's style of play. Aggressive. Daring. Intelligent. But the most telling word would have to be "provocative." She didn't play the ball. She played the man. *Him.* When he moved, she moved. Her smile never wavering, her eyes on his waist in order to see instantly which way he would go almost before he knew it himself, she used every part of her body to block, guard and distract him.

As he drove toward the basket he couldn't clear his mind of the fact that her left hand rested lightly on his spine while her right hand was all but shoved in his face. When he set himself to take a shot, she waved her arms and jumped up and down within inches of him, her ponytail whirling about like a propeller.

He couldn't take a step without feeling that they had somehow been glued together. And when she had the ball, she used her hips, shoulders and back to great advantage as she all but pushed him out of her way.

In short, she played basketball like a man. If she had been a man, Blake would have known how to defend against her. But Sydney was a woman. Boy, was she a woman. And his defense—along with another layer of his *defenses*—all but crumbled under the assault.

Blake and Pete won the first game by one point and didn't spot Sydney and Paul—who elected to stay on his sister's team—any points in the second game.

"I can't believe we lost!" Pete said fifteen minutes later as he sat beside Blake and Paul on the edge of the court, a wet towel draped over his head. "I knew Syd was good but I didn't think she was that good. She really had you going there, Blake. I would have run her over if she tried some of those moves on me."

Sydney stood in front of them, grinning. "And that's the difference between Blake and you, my darling brother. Blake is a gentleman."

Blake looked up at Sydney. Her hands were on her hips as she ran through a few basic cooling-off exercises. Her smooth, tanned skin gleamed with perspiration, and small ebony curls had escaped the headband to cluster around her forehead and cheeks.

He swallowed hard, trying to ignore the enticing way her damp tank top and shorts clung to her slim body as she breathed heavily, trying to recapture her breath. A gentleman? Right. Sure he was. If, that is, a gentleman could be allowed to drag Sydney behind the nearest clump of bushes and kiss her until her headband melted.

In the end, Blake decided to ignore the question, and rose to look down at the twins. "Anyone for ice cream? My treat. As the loser, it's the least I can do."

As the boys scrambled to their feet and headed toward the boardwalk, Sydney went up on tiptoe and whispered into Blake's ear. "Just in case you're feeling downhearted, I think I should tell you that I played basketball in both high school and college."

Blake looked down at her. "That explains your shooting ability, Sydney. Now tell me who taught you to tease a man half out of his mind."

Sydney shook her head so that her ponytail swatted him on the arm. She seemed to be laughing at some private joke. "Ah, Blake, nobody taught me that. I'm a woman, remember? Some things, it seems, just come naturally. Come on. I'll race you to the boardwalk!"

Blake hesitated as Sydney took advantage of his startled look to get a head start on him—again—but he only smiled. He was beginning to expect it.

He had already learned that there was no way he could remain in Ocean City for the summer and avoid Sydney.

He also knew that he no longer wanted to avoid her. That left him only one question to answer—what was he going to do about it?

Chapter Nine

Blake was working. He sat at his desk, the one that now faced the wall, and worked for three hours each morning and another two hours each afternoon. In between basketball games with the twins, and early morning walks on the beach with Sydney, and evening strolls along the boardwalk people watching, as she termed it, he sat at his desk.

He sat there and worked on his play. It was unbelievable how much work he was getting done. Certainly he was a lot further now than he had been when he first came to Ocean City.

And his work was better. Odd as it seemed, now that he was working *and* playing, his work had improved, along with his output. He had even added a casual love interest for his protagonist, and as long as he could find some way to kill her off in the third act, he believed it might work out.

The woman in the play bore a great resemblance to Sydney, both physically and in personality, but that also did not come as a great shock to Blake. Sydney seemed to be infiltrating his entire life, including his work.

No matter what he did, no matter where he looked, he felt himself thinking about her and saw things that reminded him of her. Thinking about her had quite naturally led to writing about her, and he sometimes wondered if he was in danger of falling in love with his creation, if not with the inspiration for that creation.

If what Blake and Sydney had going for them was a typical summer romance, he was now a firm proponent of the institution. But September had better come soon. September, or Act Three. One way or another, he knew he had to get Sydney Blackmun out of his system before she left Ocean City to return to being a professional student, leaving her projects—the bed-and-breakfast and her summer love—behind.

And that was what he wanted. He had come here to write, not to fall in love. Sydney was a delightful diversion, but he didn't need the complication of falling in love, really in love, with the wrong woman a second time.

He looked at his watch and saw that he should be heading for the shower. He had promised Sydney he'd go with her to the concert at the Music Pier. He switched off the power to his electric typewriter, reminding himself yet again that their relationship was nothing more than a summer romance.

Of course, he thought, testing his chin with his fingertips, deciding he needed a shave, that didn't mean he couldn't enjoy himself while it lasted.

Sydney sat on the edge of her chair, looking over the program for that night's performance of the Ocean City Pops orchestra. She looked at Blake, so handsome and clean-shaven in his crisp white shirt and navy slacks that she suddenly wished all the other people off the Music Pier so that they could be alone.

"Oh, look, Blake, they're doing a Leonard Bernstein medley," she said as he stood beside her, looking up at the stage. "I adore *West Side Story,* don't you? Natalie Wood's waist was so tiny in that white gown when she did that scene on the fire escape. I cry buckets every time I see the movie."

Blake settled into the chair next to Sydney's, his program still folded in his hand. "Let me get this straight. Do you cry over the music, the movie or the size of Natalie Wood's waistline?"

She laughed, relaxing against the back of the folding chair. "All of the above, I suppose. I hope you don't mind sitting this far out on the pier. You don't hear as many of the sounds coming in from the boardwalk, and the waves breaking beneath us lend a romantic touch, don't you think?"

"I think that I'm still trying to assimilate the idea that we're actually going to hear an orchestra perform on a pier reaching out into the Atlantic Ocean. And you tell me they do this throughout the summer season?"

Sydney nodded. "It's one of the main attractions of the island, silly. After all, Ocean City is touted as a family resort. It has rides for the kiddies, games for the teenagers and great music for everybody."

Blake looked at Sydney's animated face and shook his head. "You aren't hiding anything from me, are you, Syd? I mean, you didn't sign up with the Ocean City Chamber of Commerce when you bought Sydney's Folly, did you?"

Sydney dropped her chin to her chest for a moment, then beamed up at him. He was right, of course. She *was* overdoing it. But it was becoming increasingly difficult to talk to him without saying things, personal things having to do with the way she felt when they were together—dangerous things she knew she shouldn't say.

"Sorry, Blake. It's just that I'm an Ocean City convert, ever since Mom and I came here one November when I was thirteen."

"November?" Blake asked. "Shouldn't you have been in school?"

Her emerald eyes sparkled with mischief, happy for the diversion. "Picked up on that, did you? Let's see. If I was thirteen, that had to be Miss Potter's School. Yes, that was the one. I was expelled." She looked directly at Blake, her face suddenly solemn. "I was a bit of a handful at that age."

Blake laughed out loud, slipping his arm across the back of her chair. "And you think you're better now?" he shot back swiftly, just as the lights went down, so that Sydney couldn't answer him. Instead, she just leaned her head against his shoulder when the

Bernstein medley was announced, took a deep breath, taking in the masculine scent of his after-shave, and smiled contentedly to herself when he didn't move away.

The concert put Sydney in a strange mood, as if her whole body was one taut bundle of nerves and she needed to run, or shout, or in some other way try to dispel this feeling of coiling tension.

Once the lights had come up and they were back on the boardwalk she had to fight down an almost overpowering urge to kick off her shoes, take Blake by the hand and run down the steps to dance in the waves on the beach—which would be great fun, as she had purposely worn a full-skirted sundress that all but screamed for a little wave chasing.

Or she could be equally happy dragging Blake into the nearest candy shop, to indulge herself in some rich chocolate-mocha fudge. They could eat it as they sat on the steps leading down to the beach and guessed which of the incoming waves would break the hardest against the Fifth Street jetty. No. That was too tame.

They could go back to Sydney's Folly the way they did most evenings, where the boys were already installed in front of the television watching a baseball game, and sit on the back porch sipping lemonade while she played some of her favorite tapes for him.

She dismissed that idea almost immediately. In this mood, the last place she should be was sitting alone in the dark with Blake.

But she realized at last that it didn't really matter what they did, as long as they did it together.

The only other thing Sydney was sure of was that she didn't want to say good-night.

Then, out of the corner of her eye, she spied the antique merry-go-round at the boardwalk playland, and her mind was made up at once.

"Come on, Blake," she urged, pulling him by the hand. "If we hurry we can get outside horses, the ones that go up and down. They're working the brass-ring box tonight!"

Blake pulled her to a halt in the middle of the boardwalk. "Let me get this straight, Syd," he said, seemingly oblivious to the crush of people trying to make their way around them. "You want me to ride around in circles on a plaster horse, trying to catch a fake brass ring?"

"And you have a problem with that? No, of course you don't." Sydney tilted her head to one side and grinned up at him. "Come on," she said, tugging on his hand once again, "or we'll have to wait until the ride stops again."

"Oh, and that would be tragic, wouldn't it?" Blake responded wryly, pulling a face. "I guess we'd better hurry, then. Should I push that little redheaded kid out of your way, or do you want to just leapfrog over him?"

"Very funny, Blake. Now, come on. You'll love it. I promise!"

A moment later he was astride a large plaster palomino while Sydney effortlessly lifted herself onto a ferocious-looking black steed that she quickly told Blake was her personal favorite.

The calliope struck up a brisk Sousa march and the crowded merry-go-round slowly groaned to life. Round and round it went, with Sydney holding on to the reins with one hand as she stretched out as eagerly as the noisily shouting children on the ride, all hoping to catch the brass ring.

The merry-go-round picked up speed, the calliope switching to a rendition of "Pop Goes the Weasel," and Blake seemed to lose any remaining inhibitions. He began singing along with the music as Sydney looked back at him over her shoulder, feeling as carefree as any three-year-old.

As the happy shrieks of the children, the overpowering, tinny-sounding music and the cool night ocean air combined to wash away any lingering tension he had harbored from his last session at the typewriter, Blake let out a loud cowboy whoop and leaned over the palomino's head to leer laughingly at Sydney, pretending to urge the horse into a gallop.

All too soon the ride was over. He dismounted and went to help Sydney down, just to have her wave the brass ring in his face. "Look, Blake. This means I can ride again, *free!*"

"Do you want to ride again?"

Sydney looked at him closely, her emerald eyes dancing mischievously, before handing the brass ring to a freckle-faced girl no older than five, who immediately ran to her mommy to show her what "that nice lady gave me."

"I'll take that as a no," Blake said, his hand at Sydney's elbow as he steered her back onto the boardwalk through a maze of children and baby strollers. "I hate to admit this, but that was a lot of fun. I haven't been on a merry-go-round since I was a kid."

"I can understand why. I noticed that your feet were dragging on the ground when the horse moved down to its lowest point," Sydney said, laughing. "You know, I've seen signs that say a person must be above a certain height to go on a ride, but it never occurred to me that someone could be too tall for one."

Blake walked over to the railing, away from the noise of the crowd, and stood looking down at the incoming tide. "That's it, Syd. Pick on me. I was always the tallest in my class, even in grade school, so I'm used to it. My younger cousins used me for a tree when we played hide and seek. But now that I don't play basketball? Well, now I'm just tall."

Sydney grabbed at his arm, turning him toward her. "Which one of those featherbrained little monsters said that to you? It's bad enough that I teased you, but—oh, never mind. I'll kill them both. I'm an equal-opportunity child beater when it comes to those two. I warned them not to—"

"The boys didn't say anything, Syd," Blake answered calmly, "although I couldn't blame them for saying it—which I take it they did, to you. Smart boys. I think of it myself every time I'm in a hotel and try to fit myself onto a regular-length bed. And every time I go to buy a suit and have to pay more for it because of my size. And every time I have to bend myself in half to get into a car, or get a backache trying to dance with a woman half my size."

Sydney moved herself closer to him, measuring the top of her head against his shoulder. "Would you get a backache dancing with me?"

"No," he answered, slipping an arm around her waist. "No, I wouldn't. It would seem you have other advantages, besides being a great official tour guide to all the hot spots in Ocean City."

"We aim to please," Sydney rejoined cheerfully, slipping her arm around his waist and pulling him away from the railing. "I'm not ready to go home. Do you want to walk on the beach? We're not really supposed to this late at night, but if we go down closer to Delancey Place we can get away with it."

Stopping only to remove their shoes, they were soon walking along the shoreline, the light cast by the full moon making it easy for them to see their way as they walked in the general direction of Atlantic City, the lights of the casinos standing out garishly against the night sky.

"Tell me more about your play," she said after a long, comfortable silence during which she had allowed herself to luxuriate in the mere presence of this man she was finding more indispensable to her happiness with each passing day. "You barely even told Wilbur about it, now that I think of it. All I know is that you're adapting it from a short story."

"What do you want to know about it?"

Her head burrowed even farther into his shoulder, fitting so well she found herself thinking that his long, lean body could have been fashioned especially for her comfort. "I don't know. Everything, I guess. What time period is it set in—what era? Is it one of those talky plays, or is there a chance it could be put to music? Musicals are very big right now, you know, and since *Phantom* and *Les Misérables,* I doubt any subject could be considered too serious to be done in the form of a musical.''

"My play is *not* a musical," Blake answered, trying not to laugh.

"All right," Sydney conceded. "It didn't hurt to ask. Let me try again, okay? Honestly, this is like pulling teeth. I've met lots of writers, but you're the first one who didn't talk reams about his work at the mere drop of a hint." She bent down, picking up four small stones. "Here—I don't have any pockets. Will you keep these for me?"

She placed the stones in his palm and he looked down at them, frowning. "What are these for? You're not panning for gold or anything, are you, Syd?"

"Don't be silly. I'm going to keep them for remembrance. When I'm having an especially good time, or want to remember a place, I pick up things for remembrance. You do still have my copy of tonight's program from the Music Pier in your pocket, don't you?"

He turned her in his arms so that they were facing each other. "For remembrance, huh? Does that mean you've got a closet full of hotel ashtrays and towels somewhere in Sydney's Folly?"

Sydney frowned, because Blake wasn't getting the point. "Now, what would I want with those? I don't steal. I keep things for remembrance. You know what I mean—ticket stubs, old plane tickets, play programs, dried bouquets—''

"Hold it, Syd. Back up a minute. The programs and bouquets I can understand, but you keep *stones* for remembrance?"

She nodded furiously, then bent to pick up several more small sand-wet pebbles and held them out to him, eager to explain. "Aren't they pretty? They come in all sorts of colors, although they aren't quite as bright once they're dry, which is why I oil them with a little vegetable oil—like you do colored Easter eggs— to keep them shiny. And little shells, too, for variety. It's a tradition Mom started our first year in Ocean City. We pick some up—a half a dozen or so—nearly every time we're on the beach. Each year we find an especially pretty glass jar, and by the end of the season we've filled it to the brim with our remembrances of the things we've done and the people we've met. I've got two shelves of jars at home."

"You've got two shelves full of jars filled with shells and pebbles. You've labeled them, of course, just so that you can keep your remembrances straight. What's the label going to be on this year's jar, Syd—Blake Mansfield?"

Sydney felt suddenly nervous, noticing a slight edge had entered Blake's voice. He was talking as if she had a man's name for every jar in her collection. She shook her head, dismissing the thought as ridiculous. He couldn't have meant that. If Blake thought that way about her he wouldn't still be standing here, looking down at her so intently, and with that sweet, enticing smile on his face.

"I don't have to label the jars," she said at last. "They're for my *memories,* not some sort of fact files.

It's enough to see the jars and know that they represent happy hours, happy days. Do you understand now? Honestly, Blake, and you call yourself a writer. Don't you have any soul?"

This last was an out-and-out taunt, a dare—and she had no intention of backing away.

"Soul, is it, Syd?" she heard him question, as he gathered her—most willingly—against his length. "I'll show you soul."

Sydney giggled, happy again because he was happy, and more than willing not to ask any more questions. She was on the beach with Blake, the moon was shining on the ocean, and the time for talk had passed. It was time to enjoy the moment.

"Oh, Blake." She sighed dramatically, her fingers splayed against his shoulders as she batted her long eyelashes at him, "you're *so* masterful!"

"Oh, Sydney," Blake responded just as theatrically, tightening his grip by running his fingers through her long black hair and holding her head steady, "you talk *so much!*"

They had kissed before, but this time was different. This time they had the memories of the music on the pier and their ride on the merry-go-round behind them. Yet were those behind them? They both heard music. They both felt as if the world had suddenly gone still, and they were whirling around and around, locked firmly in each other's arms.

It was everything a romantic moment could be, complete with sand, sea and stars. They could have stayed on the beach all night, with the small wavelets tickling their bare feet while the warm ocean breeze played around the hem of Sydney's sundress.

They could have, except for the intervention of one of Ocean City's Beach Patrol's finest, who came up to them and politely cleared his throat before asking them to please move on.

After walking home arm-in-arm, giggling like schoolchildren who had been caught filching apples from a neighbor's tree, and after saying a lingering good-night to him outside her door, Sydney suddenly sobered, realizing that, once again, Blake had neatly avoided telling her anything about his play.

Two days had passed since Blake's interlude with Sydney on the beach; two days during which his progress on the play had rapidly degenerated from Full Ahead to Full Stop.

His growing dissatisfaction with his lack of concentration, combined with the knowledge that Sydney had been curiously unavailable for the entirety of that same forty-eight hours, had him heading for the beach to witness the Great Sand-sculpting Competition without so much as a backward look at his typewriter.

The competition had begun several hours earlier and had heated up by the time Blake descended to the beach to find Sydney lying on her back in a short-legged sand chair, her honey-tanned, yellow-striped-bikini-clad body glistening with a liberal application of sunscreen.

She was wearing earphones as she listened to one of her tapes, and had covered her face with an enormous straw hat, but he picked her out of the crowd almost immediately—a thought that staggered him, once he considered exactly what that meant.

After quietly depositing his towel, thongs and glasses beside her belongings, Blake took off for the ocean, determined to cool himself down, although he hadn't really been warm until he had spied Sydney. He ran into the water, dove through the waves into deeper water, and swam back and forth parallel to the beach for a good ten minutes, his arms and legs cutting through the sea almost without effort.

He emerged from the water, only partially refreshed, saw that Sydney was still hiding beneath her hat, and took up his towel and walked over to the judging area to see how the twins were doing. It had been pointless to do anything else, for Sydney seemed not to have moved a single muscle while he had been gone. When she worked, she worked, Blake concluded, rubbing his hair dry with a corner of the towel. When she played, she played. And when she rested, she *rested!*

"Did you see Syd, Blake?" Paul asked as Blake approached. "All she did was pester us with her harebrained advice and then go conk out over there on her chair. Some moral support, huh?" The boy, who had been kneeling in the sand, sat back on his haunches, wiped his sandy hands on his swimming trunks and grinned up at Blake. "So—what do you think? We thought up a new idea last night."

The sculpture was a strange sort of relief, with the six-foot-long sea creature rising out of the sand rather than appearing to have been built on top of it. Details such as the large, bulging eyes and long, stringy hair had been formed by adding shells, small pebbles and clumps of seaweed to the sculpture, and it looked remarkably professional, in a bizarre eleven-year-old-boy sort of way.

"Not bad," Blake said, and meant it.

"Hey, who said you could take a break?" Blake had turned to see Pete trudging toward them through the soft sand, struggling to keep from spilling two nearly overflowing buckets of seawater. "Do I have to keep my eye on you every minute?"

"Oh, yeah? And who made the last five trips for water, huh? Answer that, you knock-kneed dweeb!"

"If I'm a dweeb, you're a dweeb," Pete shot back hotly. "We're identical, remember?"

Blake stepped back, carefully putting himself safely out of range in case the boys decided to come to blows.

Paul stood up to go chin-to-chin with his brother. "Is that right? Then how come *this* dweeb knows that the sculpture is done—and we don't need any more water?"

Pete looked at the sand sculpture, and then back at his brother. "Hey, what do you know? How about that. It's perfect. Well, if we don't need any more water, what am I supposed to do with these two buckets?"

Shrugging, Paul idly suggested Pete simply pour the water onto the nearby sand, but Blake could see that his brother wasn't listening.

Inspiration had struck the twin who wanted to play for the New York Yankees.

"Look at her, Paul," Pete said, motioning toward Sydney. "A fat lot of help *she's* been. But you know what, bro? I'll bet she's really hot, lying there in that blazing sun all day. Poor Sydney. What do you say we cool her off?"

"Um, guys," Blake felt obliged to say, "do you think that's fair? I mean, Sydney's been working pretty hard these past couple of days, hasn't she? Maybe she needs her rest?"

"Working?" Paul jeered. "Is that what you call it, Blake? All we've seen her do is dance around the house, singing. When she isn't *reading,* that is." He winked at his brother.

Pete's eyes narrowed as he walked up to Blake and jutted out his chin. "She was reading a magazine full of pictures of brides, Blake," he said confidentially, winking at his brother. "Yeah, that's it—*brides.*"

Blake looked down at Pete, and then over at Paul, who was already solemnly nodding his head. "Brides need *grooms,* Blake," Paul pointed out unnecessarily.

Blake then looked across the expanse of sand to Sydney. He looked at her long, inviting body, which he had recognized without seeing her face.

He thought about Sydney's Folly, the project she had set herself for the summer—the sort of hare-brained adventure she could afford to play at or desert, depending on her mood.

He thought of his script, his hard work, lying on his desk untouched for nearly three days, the play she had tried to maneuver Wilbur Langley into reading.

He thought of the peace and freedom he had known until coming to Ocean City to find a black-haired goddess doing a war dance on her front porch.

Mostly, he thought of her stones for remembrance—and the way she seemed to so conveniently divide her life into seasons, playing the summers away, dabbling in a light summer romance to help pass the time, before going off in the fall to play at being a student.

That was the impression he had gotten, wasn't it—the impression she had given him? That was the conclusion he had drawn, the conclusion he had silently agreed to honor. A summer romance. Nothing more.

But bridal magazines? How did those figure into it? Nobody had said anything to him about changing the rules.

And that was when Blake, by way of stepping back three paces and keeping his mouth shut, helped to score one for the male of the species in the battle of the sexes.

He watched from the sidelines as the twins, each carrying a full bucket, tiptoed slowly across the sand toward Sydney's still form.

"Stay awake..." Pete intoned softly, quoting one of the roadside signs that lined the Atlantic City Expressway.

"Stay alert..." Paul continued seriously, although his lively young face was split with an unholy grin.

"... *Stay alive!*" they shouted together as, simultaneously, they lifted their buckets and dumped the contents on the unsuspecting Sydney.

"You monsters!"

The straw hat went east.

The earphones went west.

And Sydney headed straight for her brothers.

There wasn't a single square inch of her body that remained dry, and Blake knew it because he was enjoying his not-so-innocent-bystander view very much.

The twins separated, Paul heading for the safety of the boardwalk, while Pete, turning to make teasing faces at his sister, took off for the ocean, Sydney hard on his heels.

She caught up with him just as he was about to dive through the waves, and the two of them plunged into the ocean together. When they resurfaced on the other side of the wave, Sydney immediately dunked her brother's head under the surface and swam away.

Blake watched as the two frolicked about in the water, splashing each other and tossing friendly insults back and forth.

"That looks like fun, doesn't it?"

Blake glanced down to see Paul had returned to the beach. "Want to join them?" Blake asked, sensing that Paul, who had prudently chosen sanctuary on the boardwalk, was now regretting his decision.

"Yeah."

"She'll dunk you, too," Blake pointed out, his eyes once more on Sydney as she came up from beneath another wave, her long black hair plastered to her skull as she looked about for her brother, mayhem clearly on her mind.

"And you," Paul said. "Sydney loves a good water battle. Blake—we were only kidding about the magazines. We just wanted you on our side. Syd's been busy painting a couple of the guest bedrooms because the furniture's going to start arriving next week. Honest.''

"I knew that," Blake lied quickly. He felt foolish for a moment, then realized that he also felt something else. He felt vaguely disappointed. It was a frightening discovery. "What are we waiting for?" he asked Paul, already taking off his glasses, hoping the saltwater might help restore his senses. "Let's go get 'em!"

They spent most of the remainder of the afternoon in the water, alternately jumping the waves and riding on the twins' bodyboards, Sydney's infectious good humor making a party out of what had been only another lazy summer day at the beach.

The twins' sea monster took first place in the Junior Division of the sand-sculpting contest, which had been no mean feat, considering their competition, and Blake helped them celebrate by treating everybody to ice cream before they held an impromptu paddleball tournament in the shallow water near the shore.

When they finally, reluctantly, gathered up their belongings to return to Delancey Place for dinner, Blake saw Sydney picking up several small stones and stuffing them into her beach bag.

He had to fight down the urge to gather up some memory reminders of his own.

Chapter Ten

"Mom? Hi!" Sydney switched the telephone to her left ear so that she could use her right hand to continue stirring the wallpaper paste that sat in a bucket next to her on the floor. "What's the matter? I didn't expect to hear from you again so soon. Or didn't your undercover agent cross all the *T*'s and dot all the *I*'s on his report to you?"

Sydney held the telephone away from her ear for a few moments while her mother, seldom at a loss for words, delivered a short, pithy lecture on the rights and responsibilities of a caring parent—especially a parent who had entrusted her two young sons into the care of a young woman who had dragged home more than a few unorthodox characters in her time.

"Sorry, Mom," Sydney apologized, grimacing as her mother's dart hit home. "I was younger then, though, and Sasha seemed like a nice enough guy, even if he did wear that weird earring. How was I supposed to know his idea of performance art was to slap mud all over himself and run all but buck naked through our living room while you and Adam were giving that fancy dinner party for those completely humorless people from the National Endowment for the Arts committee? Besides, I hear Sasha's making big bucks in Soho right now, and laughing all the way to the bank.''

Sydney listened for a moment more, then added, ''Yes, Mom, I remember Millicent as well. Who could forget her? As a matter of fact, I got a letter from her just the other day. Millie's in Hollywood now, writing for some Saturday morning cartoon show. She was just a little overzealous, locking you in the bathroom like that until you agreed to read her manuscript. Artistic people *can* be a little eccentric, you know. I mean, look at you, Mom. Much as we all love you, you do have your little ways about you.''

Once more Sydney prudently held the telephone away from her ear, dropping the brush into the wallpaper paste so that she could smother her laughter as Courtney Blackmun protested that the only eccentricity *she* had ever harbored had been an illogical refusal to send her firstborn to a strict military school.

''Okay, Mom,'' Sydney said, picking up the brush again, ''I give up. I've had some weird friends. Not bad friends—just weird ones. But tell me—did Wilbur think Blake was weird? *Ah-ha!* Just as I thought. Wilbur likes him, doesn't he?''

She leaned her head back against the wall. ''Plague and Pestilence like him, too, if you can consider that an endorsement. They're suffering from major cases of hero worship, when you get right down to it. You're just jealous because you can't be here to give Blake the official Blackmun-Richardson seal of approval. Admit it, Mom. I'm all grown up now. I haven't done anything even vaguely terrible in years, now have I?''

Sydney smiled, as her mother, who had always been her best friend, confessed to feeling left out and asked to hear more about Blake.

"I think he could be really important to me, Mom," Sydney answered slowly, her emerald eyes turning rather misty. "It didn't start out that way, but now—well, now I don't know. Don't faint when I say this, Mom, but for the first time in my life I'm actually feeling a little insecure. I've read all your books, even if I've never made time for much in the way of personal experience when it comes to romance. I never understood how any one man could have such an impact on a person, especially in just this short time. I don't want to do anything stupid and lose him."

She took a deep breath and let it out slowly. "So, hey, Mom, do you think you and Pops might be coming home soon?"

Sydney stood back and allowed Blake to enter the bathroom. "Now tell me, what do you think?"

Blake looked around the large room, which had been furnished in deliberate antiques, complete from the oversize claw-footed tub to the marble pedestal sink. "You did this?" he asked at last, knowing his tone to be faintly incredulous.

Sydney leaned against the doorjamb, her arms crossed against her waist. "I didn't do the plumbing, if that's what you're referring to, although I did pick it all out. The original stuff was past saving. Really prehistoric. No, I mean, what do you think of the wallpaper job? Loving hands at home, you know."

He shifted his inspection to the walls to see they had been covered with a floral design paper that, unbeknown to him, was an original Laura Ashley print. He backed into the hallway, his inspection of the handiwork completed. "Nice job, Syd," he told her sincerely. "You even remembered to cut the paper around all the doors and windows. Or are there supposed to be three windows in that room?"

"You really like it?" Sydney's face glowed with pleasure. "There are a couple of rough spots behind the bathtub, where the pattern doesn't exactly match, but I doubt anyone will get down on their hands and knees to look for them. All in all, I'd say I did fairly well for my first time out of the box. As a matter of fact, Blake, I'm immodest enough to tell you that I'm pretty darn proud of myself!"

They retraced their steps to the side porch, where Blake saw the inevitable pitcher of lemonade waiting for him. The strange thing was, he found himself beginning to actually like the stuff. "I thought you were going to paint the rooms."

She nodded, pouring them each a glass of lemonade. "I am. I did. You mean, you didn't notice? Everything's painted now, except for the hallway and the solarium. I'm only using wallpaper in the bathrooms, and then again as borders around the ceilings of the other rooms."

She took a sip of lemonade. "Well, not all the rooms. In the dining room I'll use a wallpaper border at the same height as a chair rail would normally be placed. I've ordered all the drapes at this special store that sells matching wallpaper for all its patterns. I think it'll be a great look, semi-Victorian, yet functional, and at only a fraction of the work. Wallpaper can be messy, you know. I nearly glued Pete to the bathroom wall by mistake before he made his getaway. So—how's the writing coming along?"

Blake threw back his head and laughed aloud. "You never give up, do you, Syd? You talk about one thing—like the wallpaper—but at the tail end of the conversation you slip in yet another question about my play. You're like a senator sticking a pet project on the end of a bill up for a vote in Congress, hoping to get it passed without anyone the wiser."

"I am not!" Sydney protested, then grinned. "Okay, okay. So I am. Only, I guess those senators have it down to a fine art that still escapes me."

She pulled her legs up onto the chair to sit crosslegged and leaned toward him, instantly putting him in mind of a small child about to beg to be taken to the zoo. "But how come you're the one laying all the ground rules? We can't talk about anything heavier than the chance of rain during our morning walks— not that I'm complaining, because I like quiet walks along the beach. We can't talk about the play at night because there's too much going on while we're on the boardwalk, what with the boys forever challenging you to miniature golf or that basketball game at the arcades.

"Come on, Blake, I'm curious. No, correct that. I'm nosy! I'm all but dying with curiosity. I've even lain awake at night, thinking up clever new ways to get you to tell me about it, and wondering if you're deliberately driving me to distraction. Just give me a hint, okay?"

Blake looked at Sydney, who was dressed in her usual shorts and top, her healthy, tanned complexion scrubbed so that it actually shone, her heavy black hair tied into two ponytails behind her ears.

She looked as youthful as a teenager.

She held all the allure of a mature young woman.

And she had the tenacity of a bulldog!

He held up his hands in surrender. "All right, all right! I give up. I can't fight you anymore. I'll tell you about the play."

She leaned forward even farther, so that he was momentarily afraid she would topple off the wicker chair into his lap. "You'll let me read it?"

Yup, Blake thought ruefully, *a bulldog. Once she got hold of you, it would be nearly impossible to shake her loose again.* He sighed and shook his head. So far, much against his inborn sense of self-preservation, he had been allowing himself to daily become more involved with and attracted by Sydney Blackmun.

All the promises he had made to himself that had to do with assuming command of this summer romance had perished unborn and unlamented. If Sydney was a hungry bulldog, he had willingly stuck out his leg to give her a better target.

He took a deep breath before giving her an answer. "No, you may not read it," he told her at last. "I'm very protective over my work in progress. What I will do is let you read the short story on which the play is based. Fair enough?"

"Eureka!" She hopped to her feet to look down on him, her eyes shining. "Let's go, I'm ready," she said eagerly, reaching down to grab his forearm. "No time like the present, right? Oh, darn it!"

Blake could hear the telephone ringing and exaggeratedly wiped at his brow in relief. "Saved by the bell," he said teasingly. "But, please, don't forget to tune in at the same time next week for the exciting conclusion of 'Sydney the Snoop.' Will she ever see Blake Mansfield's short story? Or will she be doomed to go through life forever wondering—does the story really exist? Or is it all some figment of his twisted imagination?"

Sydney looked from Blake to the open door that led to the hallway and the insistently ringing telephone and then back to him before groaning in exasperation, "Oh, stuff it!" and heading for the door. "And don't you move—unless you're going to your condo to get the magazine!"

Blake sat sipping his lemonade for a few minutes, easily overhearing Sydney as she argued with the person on the other end of the telephone about a delivery date for some furniture, silently congratulating himself for once more avoiding the subject of his play.

He wasn't quite sure why he didn't want Sydney to see it. No, that wasn't true. He knew why. He was afraid to let her read it. Afraid of her reaction to what he was sure was turning out to be an abysmal mistake, an arrogantly ignorant overappraisal of his own talent for creativity.

In short, he was afraid the play stank. Smelled. Laid like a bomb at the bottom of the deepest hole in the ocean.

And it would kill him if he looked into her eyes after she had put the pages down and saw disappointment or pity peeking out from behind her inevitable forced vocal appreciation of his work. And if that made him seem cowardly, then so be it.

Criticism he could take. Rejection he had learned to take—in many forms. But he realized with a start, the pain he'd felt at losing basketball, at losing everything that went along with basketball, was nothing compared to the pain he was sure he would feel if he ever looked at Sydney and saw the sparkle drain out of her glorious emerald eyes.

He glanced down at his watch, wondering if he could make some excuse about getting back to work and make good his escape while she was still trying to explain that she wasn't ready for delivery of *all* the furniture she'd ordered.

Blake took off his glasses and pinched the bridge of his nose between thumb and forefinger. No, that wouldn't work. She'd only follow him home, like the bulldog she was. Besides, he didn't mind if she saw his short story. It was a damn good piece of work, and he was proud of it. But once she read it, her previous efforts to see the play could only pale in comparison to the new barrage of questions she was bound to hurl at him.

Blake rose to enter the building, intending to tell Sydney he would go over to the condo and bring back the play.

But his mind changed when he saw her.

How he had missed it until this time he couldn't understand, but Sydney had actually placed a full-sized old-fashioned telephone booth in the right-rear corner of the alcove that held the staircase. Maybe she had painted it. Surely he couldn't be so blind that he'd missed a fire-engine-red phone booth with a three-foot-high lop-eared dalmatian standing guard beside it! The booth even had a stained-glass insert display-ing the word "telephone" at the top of the front panel.

She waved to him while she nodded her head as if the person on the other end of the telephone could see her. "Yes, yes, that's right. The carpets, the bedroom furniture, the kitchen and dining-room sets, the pi-ano and the billiards table. But *not* the living-room furniture, any upholstered chairs, the hat rack, the rolltop desk or any of the other office furniture. And the lamps! For pity's sake, please bring some lamps. It's time I got out of the Dark Ages. Oh, thank you. You're a wonderful man! I'll look for you bright and early tomorrow morning. Goodbye."

As she hung up the telephone, Blake stepped for-ward to put his hands on either side of the booth, ef-fectively making her his prisoner. "It sounds like you charmed that guy out of his socks, Syd. But before you might get any ideas in that direction, let me tell you that I do *not* rearrange furniture. And neither will the twins, once I explain the procedure to them, and the way you women have of wanting to see how the piano looks against the other wall—just to decide it looked better where it was."

Sydney remained seated and just raised a hand to flick at Blake's nose with the tip of her index finger. "Silly man. A lot you know. I've measured everything down to the last centimeter. I know precisely where every piece of furniture is to go. Although," she said, drawing out the word as she grinned up at him, "you may be right about the piano. I know it should be placed against an inside wall, because of the sounding board and all that stuff, but there are three inside walls in the living room. Perhaps after the deliverymen have gone you and the twins could help me—"

"You wouldn't dare," Blake said, leaning closer to her.

Suddenly she was on her feet, pulling him completely into the booth. "Would you look at that, Blake? There's still plenty of room, even though both of us are tall. Who would have believed it? You know, I've always wondered how they did that 'how many people fit in a telephone booth' stunt at college."

"Telephone booths were too tame for us. We did it with an old compact car," he said, her talk reminding him of one of his fraternity's college stunts. Sydney's body was touching his from knee to chest, and Blake couldn't seem to summon the will to back up. "I think we set a new school record of thirty-two. They didn't let me or any of the football or basketball players in, though. We would have taken up too much room."

"I've seen pictures of students in cars, and in telephone booths. They always looked as if they'd have to be surgically removed."

Sydney wiggled her body about so that she was kneeling on the small wooden seat, a movement that had her resting her hands on Blake's shoulders in order to keep her balance. "There, that made room for at least one more. But we need more people, don't we, for a real test? I wish the twins were here."

"I wish the twins were in Paris with your parents." Blake was beginning to enjoy himself. He slipped his hands around Sydney's waist. "When are they due home?"

"The twins or my parents? I'll assume you mean Pete and Paul. They're at the movies," Sydney told him, her voice still teasing, but suddenly faintly breathless as well. "I don't know exactly when they'll be back. Why?"

Blake kicked the bi-fold door shut behind him. "Because I remember another college stunt. One of the fraternities joined with one of the sororities to see if they could set a new record for the longest kiss."

Sydney's arms snaked around his neck. "Oh, really. And did they break the old record?"

Blake was enjoying himself. "No. Midterms interrupted them, or something like that. But as I wasn't allowed in the car squeeze, I was thinking I ought to get at least one chance at a world's record. What do you think?"

Sydney's smile turned his gut into a clenched fist. "I think, since you're finally going to let me read your short story, that one good turn deserves another. Do we count in our heads, or would you rather check the time on your watch?''

"A watch?" Blake lowered his mouth to within a whisper of hers. "I'd rather use a calendar," he said, then closed the gap.

Kissing Sydney was pleasurable, something Blake had learned during their first embrace. Kissing Sydney could also be dangerous, something he had discovered when they had kissed for the second time. But kissing Sydney could also be habit-forming, like his need for air, and water, and food.

She didn't just melt in his arms. Sydney was not a passive kisser. She reacted to his kisses with the same delightful enthusiasm she put into everything she did.

That enthusiasm was not without its effect.

Blake moved slightly away from her in order to slant his mouth and deepen the kiss. Once again Sydney did not react passively to his actions. Their tongues dueled deliciously as their bodies strained against each other, seeking a satisfaction that eluded them even as their passion escalated.

She fit against him as if she had been expressly fashioned by nature for just such a purpose. Her sleekly formed body carried not an ounce of superfluous flesh, yet she was soft and yielding in all the right places. Her midnight-black hair was silky and rich, and her emerald eyes seemed to hold all the mysteries of the universe.

She was all the seasons wrapped into one, possessing the moonlit sparkle of winter snow, the fiery passionate colors of fall, the eternal promise of spring and the wildest summer heat.

Never before had he wanted a woman so much. The more she gave, the more he wanted, and the more he wanted, the more she, in turn, demanded from him. If it were possible, and oh how he wished it were, they would merge together and become one body, one mind, one heart, and he would never again have to say good-night to her and return to the moonlit beach to walk and think and dream alone.

With the sane portion of his brain—admittedly, at that moment, a very small portion—Blake remembered where they were and who they were.

He and Sydney were taking a step, even if they were confined within the booth and it could only be a figurative step.

They were deepening their relationship by deed and thought. They might not have talked about it, or even pretended to consider the consequences, but they were moving daily toward that fatal word, commitment. Their relationship might have begun as a convenient, almost mandatory summer romance, but nobody seemed to have explained the rules to their hearts.

What they were doing was wonderful, probably even inevitable for two people who had so much in common, but their timing was lousy, in more ways than one.

"Syd." Blake willed his hands back into neutral zones. He pulled away momentarily, only to gently press her head against his shoulder. "I think the telephone should ring again."

"You mean it isn't?" Sydney questioned, her voice slow and faintly husky as she placed feather-light kisses along his bare neck. "Funny. I hear bells ringing somewhere, Blake. And when I close my eyes, I think I can see stars."

Blake laughed, the sound a low rumble deep in his chest. "Maybe we're running out of oxygen in here," he suggested wryly. "But you know what I mean. If this telephone booth were any larger, you and I could be in big trouble. As it is, I think we'd better get out of here."

Sydney pulled back to look up at him. "But what about the world record? I may be wrong, but I think it's still July."

"Maybe we'll try again in August," Blake said, opening the door and carrying Sydney out into the hallway where he held her until she could regain her balance. "But for now, I think we'd better take it easy."

The look on Sydney's face nearly destroyed him. Her honesty hit at him with the force of a wave at high tide. "Why? You were enjoying it as much as I. You know, Blake, there are times you remind me of my mother, which I told her when she called this morning to make sure I wasn't falling for some weirdo who'd escaped from prison to take up residence next door."

"Your mother?" Blake interrupted. "Syd, what we were doing just now couldn't possibly have reminded you of your mother."

"Don't interrupt while I'm trying to make a point! Something is going on between us, Blake. Something has been going on between us since the first day we met. Am I reading you incorrectly, and is this just a summer fling for you? Or do you think I see you as nothing more than another project, like Sydney's Folly? And don't try to deny it. I've seen that look in your eyes time and again. When we first met, you thought I was a flirt, out for a good time—and you were the one to ask me if I was working for my merit badge when I tried to help you. I may come on as a bit of a scatterbrain, as Mom reminded me this morning, but I'm a reasonably intelligent adult. I know what I'm doing.''

He leaned down to kiss the tip of her nose. ''That's good to hear, Syd. I'm glad one of us does. Now, come on, I can hear the boys out front. We'll have to take this up again later.''

''Oh, goody! All of it, Blake?'' Sydney teased, grabbing his arm as they walked down the hallway to the front porch, her good humor seemingly returned. ''Are we going to take up *all* of it again where we left off?''

Blake shook his head, unable to be angry with Sydney for being herself. ''What's your mother's telephone number in Paris, Syd?''

She looked up at him owlishly. ''Why would you want Mom's telephone number?''

''I was hoping she could give me a few Sydney lessons. I've done all right so far, but if we're going to advance to graduate studies, I think I could use a tutor.''

''Oh, Blake,'' Sydney said, melting against him, her eyes shining, and it was all he could do to be civil to the twins when they came bursting through the door to regale them with their story of the latest dolphin sighting at the Fifth Street beach.

* * *

The queen-size bed that had been delivered that morning was a miracle of softness compared to the narrow cot she had been sleeping on, and ordinarily Sydney would have been lying back on it, pillows all about her, luxuriating in its decadent comfort.

But not tonight. Not after a long day spent supervising the deliverymen as they nicked the newly painted walls trying to maneuver the piano into the solarium—a last-minute change in her floor plan that might or might not have been instigated by Blake's remark about the whims of women decorators.

It had been a trying day, pretending to remain calm while watching the deliverymen stumble up the curved staircase with heavy pieces of furniture, while at the same time protecting the twins from learning any new words as the workmen gave their unsolicited opinion of that same staircase.

But at last the day was over. Every rug and chair and lamp was in its proper place, and Sydney's Folly wasn't looking all that bad.

In another few weeks she'd be ready to hang out her Open For Business sign, at least a month ahead of schedule. She could only hope the delivery company wouldn't send the same men back when it came time to deliver the hot tub to the roof!

The twins had been asleep for over an hour, too exhausted to complain about missing a night on the boardwalk, and Sydney was at last free to read Blake's short story—the one she had pried from his reluctant fingers that afternoon—without fear of outside interruption.

Getting the magazine from Blake had been like pulling alligator teeth with an eyebrow tweezer, even if he had agreed the day before to let her read it. He had been as nervous as a cat on hot bricks when he had held it out to her, then withdrew it just as quickly, explaining that he had marked some of the passages and she should ignore his scribbles.

Only when she had exaggeratedly crossed her heart and hoped "to spit" had he at last given her the magazine, but then he had insisted she read it while he watched.

Having lived with her mother's reaction to having her words read in front of her, Sydney had been reluctant to agree, but she would have done almost anything to get her hands on the story.

But just as she had supposed, Blake's plan had not worked. Every time she had lifted her gaze from the page, every time her facial expression changed or she shifted her weight in the chair, Blake's eyes were on her like sand on a wet bathing suit, so that she found it impossible to concentrate.

If it hadn't been for the arrival of the deliverymen with the furniture, she was sure she would have ended up tossing him bodily over the porch rail, just so that she could read in peace.

So here she was, tucked up in bed, fresh from the shower, an open box of saltwater taffy at her side, finally reading Blake's short story, "Unintentional Foul."

She read it straight through, forgetting the box of taffy, forgetting that she had seen a light still burning in Blake's condo and decided that he was pacing the floor, fighting the impulse to come storming over to Sydney's Folly to demand she tell him what she thought of his story.

When she was done she read it through again from the beginning, her attention centering on the high-lighted areas, the places Blake must have marked for expansion.

And then she cried.

Chapter Eleven

Sydney woke to the sound of a drenching rain pelting against her curtained window. There would be no walk on the beach this morning. She burrowed back down under the light cotton covers, a relieved smile on her face. Nature had given her at least a momentary reprieve.

She turned over onto her side, sighed contentedly, pulled the covers up around her chin and immediately fell back to sleep.

Fifteen minutes later, with the insistent ringing of the doorbell blasting her back to consciousness, she realized her mistake. Blake would have waded through a monsoon, sharks circling him and coming in for the kill, to hear her opinion of his short story.

She rolled out of bed, tugging a thigh-length yellow terry robe over the Cambridge T-shirt that had served as her nightgown, and stumbled toward the stairs as

Pete stuck his head out into the hallway to order grouchily, "If that's another one of your dippy deliverymen, Syd, shoot him!" before disappearing once more into his bedroom.

"You got it, ace!" she shot back, blowing a strand of hair out of her eyes.

The smell of freshly brewed coffee, courtesy of her trusty, programmable coffee maker, met her at the bottom of the curved staircase, but the aroma was not enough to shake her brain into functioning at its usual speed.

She was tired, she was disheveled and she was still totally without a clue as to how to approach Blake about her mixed reactions to his short story.

Her self-directed anger quickly transferred itself to Blake. Maybe she *had* bugged him forever about reading his work, but did that give him the right to come banging down her door less than twenty-four hours after finally giving it to her, demanding a critique?

After all, he hadn't wanted her to read the dratted thing in the first place!

By the time she reached the front door, Sydney had succeeded in building up a rare head of steam, something inside telling her that, as in sports, the best defense is a good offense.

"*What?*" she bellowed as she pulled open the door with a flourish. He looked so adorably drenched that she longed to throw herself into his arms, but she resisted the impulse. "Is your condo on fire? Has the Coast Guard sighted an unmarked sub offshore? Did you win the New Jersey lottery? Whatever it is,

Mansfield, it had better be good. It's raining puppies out there, and you woke me up!''

Blake dripped his way into the hallway, his smile wide as he took off his glasses and wiped them on his shirt. ''And you seemed like such a morning person, Sydney. You didn't warn me that your sunny disposition was so closely connected to the sun itself. That's a shame. I went out walking without you. The beach is wonderful in the rain, even if it does play hell with the doughnuts.'' He held up a crumpled, rain-soaked paper bag as if to prove his point.

She gritted her teeth and looked down at his sand-encrusted sneakers. ''It's a pity the beach isn't equally wonderful in my hallway. You brought half of it in here with you, you know.''

''Whoops, sorry about that.'' Blake leaned against the wall as he reached a hand down to pull off his sneakers, leaving his feet bare. ''What should I do with them?''

Sydney rolled her eyes. ''Oh, Blake, don't give me openings like that. Not when I'm in a bad mood. Here—give them to me. I'll put them out on the front porch until you leave.''

''Then I am going to get coffee,'' he remarked, heading down the hallway toward the kitchen. ''Good. You know, Sydney, you'll have to work on this mood problem. You won't be allowed to bark at your paying customers just because it's raining, not unless you want them all to run screaming into the streets.''

''But you're not a paying customer,'' Sydney answered reasonably. ''Besides, you already know I'm only going to be here during the summer, when I'm not at school."

Blake took off his jacket, hanging it on the back of one of the kitchen chairs before going over to the counter to pour himself a cup of coffee. "Oh, yes," he answered, looking at her strangely. "Once Sydney's Folly is up and operational, you'll be off again until next summer. Strange how I keep forgetting that lately. So tell me, which school is it to be this year, Syd? Some trendy little university in the south of France?"

"Not now, Blake. We'll talk about that later. Besides, I already told you my school is in Fairfield. That's in Connecticut. Pour me a cup, will you?" she all but pleaded, collapsing into a nearby chair to rest her elbows on the table and her head in her hands. She had to think. She had to cudgel her sluggish brain into finding some way to approach him about his short story. "I need a caffeine hit to the brain before I can feel really awake, let alone talk about school or next summer."

A few moments later a hot, steaming cup of coffee was placed in front of her, and she heard the scrape of a chair as Blake joined her at the table. "Drink up, Syd, you look terrible. Or did I hit a nerve with that crack about the paying customers? What's the matter? I know this place has been a lot of work. Have you lost interest in Sydney's Folly already?"

Sydney sipped gratefully at the coffee, taking the time to marshal her thoughts. But Blake's barely veiled accusation stung, and she ended up by rushing into speech. "Don't be thick. Of course I haven't lost interest in Sydney's Folly. I love this place, Blake. I've enjoyed every minute I've spent working on it. It's such a concrete thing. I can look around and actually see the results of my work, done with my own hands, using abilities I never knew I possessed."

"And you've done a fine job. Like I said before, real merit-badge caliber." Blake shook his head. "Yes, another of Sydney's summer projects nearly completed."

She deposited her mug on the table with a small thud. "You're being sarcastic, Blake. You never told me you're sarcastic in the morning."

"Sorry, Syd. I was out of line. You have every right to be proud of this place."

Sydney hid the sudden, satisfied thrill that rushed through her body at hearing Blake praise her work. "But there's still so much to do. I have to hire some people to run the place, I think a retired couple I've met in town would be perfect, and then stick around a while longer, to make sure all the wrinkles have been ironed out of the operation."

She turned to him and smiled. "I've already made one small change in my plans, though, Blake. There will be one less guest room to rent, because I've decided to keep my room year-round. It's funny, but I've begun to think of this place as my home now."

Blake nodded, his expression guarded. "It must be nice, being you, living your life. But are you sure you want to keep on spending your summers in Ocean City, Sydney, collecting remembrances? I mean, you can change your mind whenever you want, go where you want, when you want."

She knew what he meant. She didn't quite know how she knew it, but she did. He was hinting that she led an aimless life, indulging herself with summer projects—and maybe even summer loves. Heaven knew, he had alluded to having that impression of her before this.

But if Blake thought he was going to goad her into an argument, he had missed his mark, for now she knew all about *him*. Besides, he had unwittingly given her the opening she needed, a way to approach him about his short story.

Sydney leaned back in her chair and looked at him levelly, her own bad mood all but forgotten as she reveled in his shift of temper. "Really pushed the wrong button this time, Blake, didn't I?" she inquired sweetly. "What's the matter with you? Jealous?"

"Jealous! Jealous of what?"

She shrugged. "I don't know. My freedom of choice—purchased with money I haven't personally earned. No, I doubt that. You might be a little envious, and I can't blame you, but I don't think you've ever lost any sleep over the fact that I'm financially comfortable. No, it's not that. And it's not that you think I'm flighty or immature, not really. You may have believed that once, Blake, but not anymore. You understand how I feel about Sydney's Folly. It's my *freedom* to do what I want, when I want, that really sticks in your craw, isn't it?"

She saw his cheeks pale beneath his tan. "I've hit on it, haven't I, Blake? It's my freedom to choose that's gotten you all worked up."

Blake was silent for a long time, long seconds during which Sydney felt herself passing through several levels of hell, before he leaned forward to peer intently into her eyes. "You've read it, haven't you? You've read my short story."

Sydney sighed, remembering how she had felt after completing "Unintentional Foul." "Yes, Blake. I've read it. Several times. Sam Everett would have given a lot to have my options, wouldn't he?"

Blake pushed his chair away from the table, stood up and crossed the room to the sink facing the window and the heavy rain that continued to fall. Placing his hands on the edge of the counter, he lowered his head before answering her. "Sweetheart," he said, his voice low and painfully weary, "Sam would have given everything he had."

Listening to his answer nearly broke her heart. But she had been right. He had unwittingly given her the key, her way to answer his question about his work—if she only dared to use it. It was now or never. Sydney took a deep breath, crossed her fingers and forged ahead. "No, Blake, he wouldn't have. He was too busy feeling sorry for himself to see an opportunity if it walked up and smacked him in the face with a flounder! Sam Everett was a jerk!"

"*What!*" Blake's voice came like a pistol shot, slamming across the kitchen to hurl itself straight into Sydney's chest. His chin jutting forward belligerently, he all but ran across the room to slap his palms on the tabletop and glare into Sydney's eyes. "Do you want to tell me what in hell you mean by that?"

Had she really thought she wanted to wrap her arms around him and comfort him? Silly girl. Now she fought the impulse to turn and head for the hills. "All right, all right," she said in hopes of appeasing him, while trying for a little comic relief at the same time. "But back off a couple of feet, will you, Blake? All that steam coming out of your nostrils is beginning to frizz my hair."

She drained the last of the coffee from her cup before speaking again. "You asked if I read your short story. I did. And maybe it isn't fair of me to comment on it, seeing as how you didn't want me to read it in the first place, and seeing as how I'm not a professional, like Wilbur, or Mom, but I *have* read it and I *have* formed an opinion, sort of, and you won't rest until I tell you that opinion—right?"

Blake ran a hand through his hair, clearly reaching the end of his rope. "Syd, you're stalling," he gritted warningly. "You're also nearly incoherent, but that's nothing new, so I guess I'm just wasting my time pointing it out to you. Now, get on with it!"

"Yes, sir," Sydney answered, sighing. "First of all, the writing is excellent!" She grinned, feeling she had scored a point by leading with what had been right about the story. "Truly excellent! It's strong, it's spare, it's totally believable. Editorially, there isn't a thing I would have done with it. You're extremely talented, maybe even gifted. Your style is very clear, very dominant and extremely powerful. I cried buckets at the end."

"But?" Blake prodded, leaning forward another fraction, her praise seeming to have skimmed over his head as he listened for what was sure to come next. "Come on, Syd, it's hanging out there, ready to pounce. Give me the 'but.'"

Sydney closed her eyes, knowing what she said now might cause Blake Mansfield to leave her life forever. "But," she went on, shrugging, the word coming out as a small squeak, "it's a pointless story."

Blake was on his feet in an instant. "Pointless? *Pointless!*"

"Yes, that's what I said," Sydney agreed, rubbing at her right ear, "although I said it about twelve decibels lower." She watched as he began pacing the kitchen floor, his right hand jabbing at the bridge of his glasses. He looked so achingly vulnerable again that she once more wanted to go to him and kiss away all his pain. His evident anger, however, kept her prudently glued to her chair.

"I guess I'd better explain what I mean—especially the 'jerk' part. That might have been a little strong," she said, sitting up straight, her hands coming into play as she gestured with them while she spoke. "Sam Everett wanted to be a surgeon. He worked for years and years, concentrating his entire being on his goal, just to have it snatched away from him when he was in that automobile accident and lost the use of his left hand."

"You can skip the pithy synopsis, Syd. I already know the story," Blake gritted, leaning against the counter.

"Don't interrupt me, Blake, please," she countered. "This is difficult enough as it is. Sam lost his dream, yes, and he mourned that loss, which is totally acceptable. You put that part across very well, by the way. My heart broke for him. But it stopped there. Sam never tried to hold on to even part of his dream. He just settled for the ashes of his dream, for the bitter memory of what was and what could have been. He turned his back on medicine completely, and on his friends, to become a commodities broker, for heaven's sake, living his life—as you said it so brilliantly in the story—speculating on the future of everything except himself. I ended the story feeling so terribly sorry for myself—and so terribly angry with him! How could he have simply *settled?*"

Blake shook his head. "Sorry for yourself? Why yourself? I don't get it. I'm the one who should be bleeding here, Syd."

Sydney rose and walked over to him. "I was sorry for myself because I knew I had to tell you the truth, that you'd accept nothing less than the truth. You'd see right through me if I lied to you, gushing about what a terrific story it was. But that doesn't really matter. What matters is that I finished the story so totally out of charity with Sam. What a waste. What a total, terrible, unnecessary waste!"

Blake looked down at her, an unnatural, cynical smile twisting one corner of his mouth. "Oh, I get it now. I forgot. You're Courtney Blackmun's daughter. What's the matter, Sydney? Didn't I give you a nice, predictable fairy-tale-romance happy ending, all tied up in pink ribbons? Sam wasn't saved by the love of a good woman and some miracle bionic hand that allowed him to return to surgery? Syd, haven't you learned that the *real* world doesn't always have happy endings?''

"No, Blake. You're the one who doesn't get it. You're writing the literature of despair, if you'll allow me to use that cliché. Sam Everett suffered, yes, but he never had the guts to take his shattered dream and turn it around, look at it from every angle and mold it into something else. He just took off, one of life's walking wounded, turning his back on his talent as well as his dream. His story has no message, no moral. It begins in the middle and ends in the middle, with nothing learned, nothing accomplished, nothing gained.''

She shook her head. "The literature of despair, Blake, is pointless. Sam was everything but human. The spark was missing.''

"And what's that spark you're talking about, Sydney? And I'm not being facetious. I really want to know.''

"Hope!" Sydney all but shouted, her arms waving in the air. "There was no hope in your story, Blake. You've highlighted places where you want to enlarge the story into a play, but you'll only be expanding the misery. You're not writing a play. You're cataloguing Sam's pain, and his stubborn unwillingness to take the lemons fate handed him and make lemonade.''

Blake laughed out loud and slapped at his forehead with the palm of his hand. "Lemonade! You use it for every occasion, don't you? I knew I hated the stuff!'' He turned to glare at Sydney, his expression anything but amused. "Now, why don't we get down to the nitty-gritty? You're not really talking about my fictional Sam Everett, are you, Syd?''

Sydney turned her head away, unwilling to meet Blake's eyes. "Well, it is fairly common knowledge that many writers, wittingly or unwittingly, often tend to be autobiographical."

Blake took hold of her elbow and whirled her about to face him. "Not this author! I am *not* Sam Everett! Contrary to your romantic ravings, I have not turned my back on any dream! I've written two dozen or more short stories, and I've never appeared in any of them. Talk about assuming things, Syd—you've taken a quantum leap this time."

She reached up a hand to stroke her fingertips along his cheek. "Have I, Blake? Have I really? Haven't you turned your back on your dream? You titled the story 'Unintentional Foul,' hardly a medical term. I've seen you with the boys. You're a talented writer, but you still haven't come to terms with your inability to fulfill your dream of a career in basketball. You love the game, really love it. Can you look me in the eyes and deny that?"

She waited, holding her breath, praying for him to speak, praying she hadn't opened her mouth only to blow her chance for happiness once and for all. For she knew now, even more than she had known last night—as she had lain in bed, crying for him and for his lost dream—that she loved Blake Mansfield with all her heart.

"You know, Syd," he said at last, his tone dull and defeated, "I never wanted you to read the story. But once you had, a simple 'it was very nice, Blake' would have done it for me. I could have lived with that. See you around, okay?"

Slowly, almost gently, as if to drag out the pain of his action, he removed her hand from his face, leaving it hanging in midair—like her hopes and dreams. Then, mumbling something about catching a chill in his wet clothing, he left without saying goodbye.

The sky wept for two days—or at least that's how Blake believed Courtney Blackmun might have described the rain that fell without letup for the next forty-eight hours.

He had been reading Courtney Blackmun's books almost nonstop, without taking time to eat or sleep, for at least twelve of those forty-eight hours.

At first skeptical, and perhaps even on the lookout for flaws and hackneyed, overblown writing, he had been immediately drawn into the lives of Courtney's characters, unable to stop until he had devoured the novel Sydney had lent him, as well as the three he had bought at one of the bookstores on the boardwalk.

And in those books, woven into and through the lives of Courtney's characters, Blake had discovered what was missing in his story of Sam Everett. No matter what their troubles, internal or external, Courtney's characters persevered. They never gave up the fight, never acknowledged defeat, never turned their backs on their dreams, no matter how tired, no matter how bruised, no matter how hard their own failings, or the world, or the people in that world, tried to keep them down.

Hope.

Courtney's characters had all clung to hope. Courtney's stories held out the tantalizing promise of hope to the reader, as well.

And Courtney's books, each and every one of them, left Blake feeling refreshed, renewed and willing to believe—if not in happy endings—that human beings have to take charge of, and responsibility for, their own happiness.

His play had been tossed into the wastebasket at midnight the first day. By dawn of the second day he had completed Courtney's books and had read his short story again, this time seeing it through different eyes—Sydney's eyes.

He saw the repressed anger, the self-pity, that stared up at him from the pages. He saw the flaws. He saw the futility. "Unintentional Foul" was just as Sydney had described it—good writing, but the literature of despair. His despair.

Only one question remained: What was he going to do about it?

Blake was a writer. He hadn't settled for being a writer. He had always planned to write—once his chance for a career with the pros had come to an end. Yet he couldn't write Sam's story, or any story, until he straightened out his own twisted, discarded, yet never forgotten dream. He couldn't write anything until he faced down the demons of doubt Sydney, and then her mother's novels, had forced him to acknowledge.

His body exhausted, his mind reduced to mush, Blake collapsed onto the couch and fell into a deep and dreamless sleep, only to awaken early the next

morning to the bright glare of the sun slicing through
the blinds and across his face. Holding a hand protectively in front of his eyes to keep the sunlight away, he
pushed himself up to a sitting position and shook his
head, trying to clear it.

There was something important for him to do this
morning. If he sat very still for a moment, he was sure
it would come back to him.

Sydney.

He sniffed derisively at his mind's knee-jerk response. Of course. Sydney. Why should this morning
be so very different? She had been his first thought
upon waking for so long that he was only mildly surprised that he had believed he needed time to think.

Sydney. On the beach just as the sun fully cleared
the horizon, running at the waves, dancing barefoot
on the sand, flirting with the sea gulls and more than
occasionally with him.

Sydney. Eating spaghetti at what he had begun to
think of as "their" Italian restaurant, and teasing the
twins with threats to steal their meatballs. Playing
miniature golf left-handed and still beating him by
three strokes. Guarding him on the basketball court
and feigning an ankle injury so that he stopped his
dribble and she could quickly steal the ball and lay one
up for two points.

Sydney. Sticking out her tongue and dangling her
body precariously on that ancient ladder as she concentrated on painting the uppermost part of one of the
porch pillars. Sitting on her favorite wicker chair on
the side porch, her legs drawn up in a lotus position,
earnestly discussing the philosophies of Nietzsche as

she drank yet another tall glass of that infernal home-made lemonade.

Sydney. Leaning her head against his shoulder as they listened to the Ocean City Pops play Bernstein. Sharing silent, knowing looks with him as, hand-in-hand, they walked the boardwalk under the stars and played at assigning occupations to the various passersby. Melting against him in the shadows beneath the pine tree in her front yard as their combined passion threatened to consume them.

He had to see her. He had to talk to her. If necessary, he had to crawl on bent knees to her, admitting his stupidity. He had been so blinded by his own disappointment that he couldn't see past it to the flaws in his badly veiled autobiographical story.

No wonder he hadn't been able to make any real headway with the play, starting about midway through Act Two. There *was* no play, and there wouldn't be one until he—the real Sam—resolved his own personal "literature of despair."

He showered, shaved and dressed in record time before heading next door, intent on getting Sydney to take a walk on the beach with him before the twins awoke and could demand equal time.

Blake enjoyed Pete and Paul. He enjoyed talking with them and he enjoyed their daily pickup games of basketball more than he could have believed he would. He enjoyed teaching the twins and the other young boys who had begun wandering onto the court the finer points of the game, and he delighted in their smiles of accomplishment when they executed his instructions correctly.

However, they had nothing to do with his plans for this morning.

He ran up the front steps of Sydney's Folly two at a time and pounded on the front door with his fist. "Rise and shine, Syd!" he called out, hoping to catch her off guard with his enthusiasm. "The beach and tides wait for no man!"

Nothing. There was no response. Blake took a moment to feel apprehensive, wondering if she would open the door only to brain him with a frying pan. After all, he had disappeared for over two days, only to show up as if nothing had happened between them, as if they had parted on the best of terms.

The door opened as Blake was raising his hand to knock again, resolved to grab Sydney the moment she appeared, kiss her senseless right there on the front porch, and damn the consequences.

"You know, Blake, my boy," Wilbur Langley said in a measured drawl, standing just inside the door, "if times were different, I would have you flogged for waking me. Oh, to have been born in those marvelous days of old. I would have been a powerful duke of the realm, of course—or no less than an earl. Dear boy, do you have any idea what time it is? Gracious, what's that? The sun? Now I know why I prefer moonlight. It's much kinder to the eyes."

"Wilbur?" Blake stepped back a pace, trying to understand. He had expected to see Sydney, or if his luck was bad, one of the twins. The last person he had expected to see was the publisher of Langley Books, his silver hair slightly mussed, dressed in striped pajamas, a burgundy silk dressing gown and soft leather slippers. "What are you doing here? Sydney said you only leave Manhattan for emergencies." He started forward, planning to enter the house. "What's wrong? Is Sydney ill?"

Wilbur gave a wide yawn, which he delicately covered with one well-manicured hand. "Ill? Heavens, no. Are you always so morbid in the morning? Why would she be ill? No, darling Sydney is far from ill. As far as Paris, as a matter of fact—probably lunching at some quaint sidewalk café even as we speak. She flew out late last night from Newark Airport, leaving me, for my sins, in charge of the Dastardly Duo. And don't frown. I'm hardly more enamored of the situation than you. A word of warning, my boy. Don't ever offer Sydney your assistance. She's not at all shy about taking you up on it.

"Tell me, Blake, I don't suppose you know how to work that coffee machine in the kitchen, do you? I left dear Clarissa behind at the condo, not wishing to injure the twins' sensibilities. Besides, Sydney refused to allow her under the same roof as her brothers. Prudish you know, like her adorable mother. Well, are you just going to stand there, gaping at me, or are you going to help me with the coffee?"

"And that's the whole, terrible story," Sydney said, collapsing against the back of the brocade couch. She looked across the oval coffee table to where her parents were sitting side-by-side on a matching couch, Adam's arm around Courtney's shoulders, the copy of Blake's short story lying in Courtney's lap. "I really put my foot in it this time, guys."

"I always said she'd never make it in the diplomatic corps, didn't I, darling?" Senator Adam Richardson remarked, smiling at his wife. They were dressed for an early dinner and the theater, and Courtney looked nearly as young as her daughter.

Courtney's emerald-green eyes narrowed slightly as she concentrated on some thought that appeared momentarily elusive. "I don't know, Adam. I've read the story. She was honest, which is never a crime, although I will say that she didn't exactly go overboard on tact. But Blake Mansfield strikes me as an intelligent man—as well as a very talented one. I think he'll come around."

"Carrying flowers or a baseball bat?" Adam countered, chuckling.

"Mom, make him stop," Sydney protested, releasing an unwilling giggle. "I flew over here for some tender loving care, not abuse."

"That, my darling daughter, was your first mistake," Courtney countered, "although it doesn't pay to go to strangers for insults when you can get them from your loving family. But no, I'm wrong. Coming here was your second mistake. You never should have left New Jersey. Whoops," she said, winking at Adam, "it was your third mistake. You never should have let Blake walk out on you like that, even if you had to tie him to a chair until you got your point across."

Adam's left eyebrow rose a fraction. "That's two of you who should never hope for a career in diplomacy. Syd," he said, turning to his stepdaughter, "Wilbur has already given Blake his seal of approval, and we trust his judgment, which is a good thing, because I don't think Blake can be equated with a stray puppy. He's more than just another one of your projects, isn't he?"

"Darling," Courtney warned. "Diplomacy, remember? We shouldn't be saying anything."

"Yes, dear, but one small lapse can't hurt," Adam responded, grinning. "Anyway, Sydney, Wilbur's judgment, combined with the terrifying knowledge that your mother and I have already agreed to keep our noses out of your life now that you're all grown-up, forces me to say this. Please don't take this the wrong way, but, Sydney Blackmun, your mother and I are on our second honeymoon. Get up from that couch and go home to Ocean City."

"Adam, Sydney came here to ask for our help," Courtney said, looking at her daughter, who was just then doing a very good imitation of a pout. "She isn't running away from her life, she's just taking a sort of emotional pit stop, in order to think things out." She smiled benevolently at Sydney. "Isn't that right, honey?"

Sydney shook her head. "Nope. I'm hiding, Mom, pure and simple. Staying out of sight until the smoke clears and hoping Blake will have come to see my point. I'm being such a chicken, I'm surprised I haven't begun to molt! Pops is right. I have to go home."

Her jaw dropped and she leapt to her feet as a sudden thought hit her. "Good Lord, Mom, what if Blake has packed up and gone? I don't even have his home address!"

"Oh, honey, I doubt he'd do that," Courtney said soothingly, but only her husband heard her, as Sydney was already on the telephone, using her precise schoolgirl French to ask to be connected with the reservation desk at the airport.

Chapter Twelve

Sydney sat at the edge of the shore as the sun slowly rose above the water, exhausted from her overnight flight across the Atlantic, the incoming tide beginning to threaten her bare toes, thinking about how the coming scene would be so much better if only it could be portrayed the way it was in the movies, rather than acted out without benefit of a script by one too-honest female and one rightfully angry male.

Her legs drawn up close to her body so that she could rest her chin on her knees as she hugged her shins, Sydney gazed sightlessly out over the ocean as, in her fertile mind, she fashioned the scene the way it *should* unfold.

Blake would see her standing near the shore—her slim form dressed in something long and white and flowing—as he descended the sea-bleached wooden steps and walked onto the beach. She would turn, her

heart pounding wildly with hope, to hold her arms out
to him, the clinging draperies of her diaphanous gown
undulating slowly in the sea breeze.

He would take a single step forward, then hesitate,
his white silk full-sleeved poet's shirt and midnight-
black leather slacks molded to his long, lean body as
he frowned, considering his next move. The gold rims
of his glasses would glint in the sunlight.

Then, like the dawn blooming in the east over the
horizon, his face would soften in a beatific, forgiving, yet incredibly sexy smile, and he would begin to
walk, then run toward her.

She too would begin to run, her spirits soaring, her
arms still outstretched, her waist-length ebony hair
flowing out behind her, her bare feet scarcely skim-
ming over the sand. In slow motion, and with violins
playing in the background, they would race across the
sand to each other.

Whoops—she stopped the imaginary film running
in her head and backed it up a few frames. She had
forgotten something. She would race toward him with
her ebony tresses floating on the wind, her ethereal
gown flowing *and* a wreath of daisies in her hair!
Heroines always wore daisy chains in their hair. It was
part of the uniform.

They would stop scant feet from each other, to gaze
soulfully into each other's eyes, wordlessly pledging
their love.

No, that was too tame.

They'd run full-tilt at each other, with Blake reaching out to catch her slim waist in his hands, lift her
high into the air and then hold her close as they spun

around and around, the full orchestra sending the music into a throbbing crescendo that blocked out the sound of the waves.

And then—ah, and then she would slide down his body until their lips met and, together, *now* gazing soulfully into each other's eyes, they would collapse onto the warm sand, to—

"Syd?"

The vision exploded into a bright nothingness as she opened her eyes. Slowly, as if her neck had forgotten how to turn, she looked up to see Blake standing beside her.

"Are you all right? I've been calling your name for the last minute. Jet lag?"

Sydney scrambled to her feet, brushed sand from the seat of the one-piece jumpsuit she had traveled in, and looked at Blake, who was clad only in a pair of cutoff denims—hardly the romantic costumes of her imagination. Yet, to her, he appeared even more sexy in the flesh than he had in her romantic vision of him.

She rushed into speech. "I'm sorry, Blake. I guess my mind was light-years away. Um, how are you?"

"Pretty good, all things considered," he answered shortly, his scrutiny of her making her feel as if, heaven forbid, he knew what she had been thinking. "Wilbur and I took Pete and Paul out for supper last night. Clarissa, too. I acted as chaperon. You weren't gone long—hardly even worth the trip. How are your parents?"

She collapsed onto the sand once more, blankly gazing out to sea. This was terrible. They were being so stiff, so stilted with each other. "They—they're

fine," she answered, nodding, then winced at her
words. "Actually, they kicked me out, or at least Pops
did. Mom was all for gathering me into her motherly
embrace and soothing my self-inflicted wounds, but
Pops wasn't having any of it. It's their second honeymoon, you know, and I wasn't invited." She looked up
at him from beneath her lashes. "Do you still hate
me?"

Blake sat down beside her, also facing the ocean. "I
didn't hate you, Syd," he said, and she could feel her
taut muscles begin to relax. "I *had* entertained fleet-
ing thoughts of chartering a fishing boat, taking you
out three or four miles and dropping you over the side
with a concrete anchor tied to your ankles—but I
never hated you."

She smiled at him. "Well, that's something, I guess.
Although I know I should have used more tact while I
was ripping apart your story. Pops said I could sin-
gle-handedly start World War Three with my big
mouth." She laid a hand on his forearm. "Anyway,
Blake, I was out of line the other day. Way out of line,
and I'm sorry."

He turned to look at her, and her stomach did a
small flip. The intensely sexy gleam in his blue eyes
was just the same as it had been in her silly daydream.
"Apology accepted, Syd, if you'll accept mine. I
overreacted, like some thin-skinned amateur." He
pulled her to her feet. "The doughnut shop should be
ready for business by now. I'll treat."

She couldn't believe it! He was going to act as if a
simple apology could make everything better, and then
just have them go on as they had been—without ex-

plaining his side of things, without truly clearing the air. Well, it wouldn't work, and she felt certain they both knew it.

"Blake, don't you think we should talk about this?" she asked, knowing she was asking for trouble at the same time. "I mean, I tore your story to shreds. I tore *you* to shreds. I badgered you forever until you let me read your work, and then I trashed it, making a personal attack against you at the same time. Are you just going to accept my apology and buy me a doughnut on the boardwalk? I don't think I can do that."

"You don't want a doughnut?" he asked, smiling down at her in a meltingly soft way that made her wish there were a nearby pillar for her to lean against before she fell down. "Too bad. I'm hungry. We'll eat now and get serious later."

She was tempted, so very tempted, to go along with him, to pretend to forget what had happened between them just four days ago. But she couldn't. She couldn't be Courtney Blackmun's daughter and just let it go until some nebulous "later" that, she had a sinking feeling, might never come. She couldn't be herself and just let it go. She and Blake could never move forward until they cleared up what had come before.

"Blake," she insisted, taking hold of his arm and deliberately leading him down the beach, away from the boardwalk, "you said you overreacted. I think I need to hear about why you think that. We have to talk—now. *Please*, Blake."

He looked back at the boardwalk, as if saying goodbye to the doughnut shop. "You're a bulldog,

Syd," he said, confusing her. "I've thought it before, and I think it now. You're a regular bulldog. All right. Let's talk."

The sun was nearly overhead by the time Sydney and Blake once again neared the Third Street beach. They had walked, and talked, and sat on one of the stone jetties, and then walked some more.

Blake felt drained, and at the same time relieved, as if some great weight he hadn't been aware of carrying had somehow slipped from his shoulders. She had been right to insist. Talking to Sydney had always been easy, but he had surprised himself by his own candor.

He had told her of his deep anger, his intense resentment, his anguished "Why me?" curses screamed into the night as the realization that his basketball career was over had finally been brought home to him once and for all.

And he had told her about reading her mother's books, and the lessons he had learned from them. Sydney had looked so smug then that he'd had to kiss her, but he really couldn't blame her for feeling proud of herself. In one swift turn of the blade, she had gone straight to the heart of his problems, whether she had known it at the time or just gotten in a lucky hit.

As a matter of fact, Blake had felt so good, so cleansed, that he foolishly brought up Joanna, his former fiancée. In a flash, Sydney went from willing listener to avenging angel.

"She *dumped* you? That's unbelievable! Why, that shallow, airheaded, miserable excuse for a female. I oughta find the slimy rock she lives under and give her a piece of my—"

Blake kissed the tip of Sydney's nose, forestalling any further description of her plans for Joanna. "Don't be too hard on her, Syd. She thought she was engaged to a future pro, not a struggling writer with a bum knee. She's done pretty well for herself. My last issue of *Alumni News* printed a small notice of her engagement to Phil Hazlett. He was co-captain of the college football team and plays in the Canadian Football League."

"Well, bully for Joanna and Phil," Sydney groused, shaking her head. "Honestly, Blake, you are the most forgiving man I have ever met. I suppose you let her keep the ring, too, even though you had given up your scholarship and could have used the money."

Blake winced. Sydney seemed able to see through him as if he were a pane of glass. "I thought I loved her, Syd, but I eventually got over it. I didn't realize how over it I really was until we talked about it today. It feels pretty good, actually. But now—considering it's nearly lunchtime and I'm starving—can't we change the subject? I think I'd like to talk about pizza."

"Oh my gosh!" Sydney suddenly grabbed at his arm with both hands, hopping up and down on the sand. "No! No, we can't change the subject. Blake, that's it! Don't you see? *That's* what's been missing!"

He punched at the bridge of his glasses as Sydney's sudden enthusiasm had nearly knocked them off. "What's it? What in the hell are you talking about?"

"Your story, of course. Gosh, Blake, try to keep your mind on the subject," Sydney said exasperatedly. "Can't you see? I told you Sam wasn't a sympathetic character, even though I knew he had been devastated by the loss of his career. He just wasn't human. I could feel sorry for him intellectually, but not emotionally. Now, introduce the *woman*—the shallow creature who turns her back on him, totally collapsing his world—and *then* he becomes human. *Then* you have a story!"

Blake was suddenly struck with inspiration. He turned to her, grabbed her upper arms as idea after idea washed over him like waves crashing onto the beach at high tide. Everything was so instantly clear that he couldn't understand why he hadn't seen it before now.

"Of course! Syd, I think you've got it! Sam wasn't three-dimensional. I never let the reader see all of him—never let them see him bleed for anything except his lost career, and not his lost dreams. Not only that, but I left the reader without hope, without showing that he had at least begun to work his way past acceptance and look toward the future."

"I said all that?" Sydney quipped, grinning. "Imagine that. Gee, I'm good, but I didn't know I was *that* good."

He released her, only to grab her hand and all but drag her along the beach. "Come on. I can't stand here on the beach all day, woman, while you pat yourself on the back. I have work to do!"

Then, just as suddenly, he stopped, Sydney almost cannoning into him. "Sydney Blackmun," he said, grabbing onto her arms once more, "you're wonderful, do you know that?"

"Of course I do, silly," she answered brightly, her wide smile nearly knocking him off balance. "I know it. *Everybody* knows it. All you had to do was ask. Now leave me here to catch my breath, and go write your play."

He pulled her toward him, grinding his lips against hers in a short, satisfying kiss, then turned to run up the beach.

Sydney wiped a tear from her eye as she turned over the last page of the now untitled short story. "It's better. *Much* better. Actually, Blake, it's wonderful."

"But—?" Blake collapsed his long, lean body against one of the front porch pillars. "Come on, Syd, I can take it. There has to be something still wrong with it, or you wouldn't be looking at me that way. I've been working night and day for three days, rewriting the entire short story before I start over on the play. Sam's girl has taken her walk after the poor guy begged her to stay, Sam has survived and decided to overhaul his life—everything is there. It wasn't easy to write, Syd. What's wrong with it now?"

Sydney laid the pages in her lap and looked up at him again. He was so dear, so sweet—and so very rumpled. "Of course I'm looking at you strangely. I haven't seen you in days, remember? You haven't slept much lately, Blake, have you? You are eating, aren't you? I wanted to bring you some dinner last night, but the twins said that it would be cruel and unusual punishment. I guess I'll never go down in history for my meat loaf.''

"Syd," Blake prompted, pushing away from the pillar to glower down at her. "You're stalling again. Now, get on with it. What's wrong with the story this time?''

Sydney's gaze slid away from his. "You're wonderful," he had told her, and then he had promptly proceeded to all but disappear from her life. He hadn't shown up at the crack of dawn for their walks on the beach. He hadn't joined the twins and her for their after-dinner strolls on the boardwalk. As a matter of fact, he hadn't even left his condo. She knew, because she had been watching.

Had she misinterpreted his kisses, the way he seemed to look at her as if she were very special to him? Today, when he had finally showed up on her doorstep, he hadn't even kissed her hello. Was it that easy for him to walk away from her? Was he going to wall himself up in the condo now, working night and day on his play? It was already the middle of July. What would happen when September came? When he left Ocean City, would he really be able to leave her behind as well?

But she couldn't ask him that question—at least not directly—no matter how desperately she needed to hear his answer. She'd have to ease into it.

"Nothing's wrong with the story, Blake. The story is really great. It delivers everything it promised. Honestly.''

Sydney laid down the neatly typed pages and rose to stand a scant foot away from him. "It's something else," she improvised quickly, inspiration striking. "Something that's been bothering me ever since I came back from Paris, ever since we met again that morning on the beach."

"Come on inside before you tell me, Syd. From the look on your face, this ought to be good." Blake deserted the porch for the house, leaving her no choice but to follow him. He walked down the hall to the billiards room, now fully furnished, picking up a cue as he went to rack up the balls. "Mind if we play while you talk? I've been cooped up for so long that now I feel as if I have to keep moving."

She selected a cue from the specially made cabinet on the wall. "You're on. Here goes, Blake. The morning I came home, that morning on the beach— you weren't angry. Remember? You forgave me, almost before I could apologize, and we went on to talk about your basketball career, as if the argument had never happened. Does that seem normal to you, Blake?"

"Really?" He questioned, laughing. Blake's firm stroke was quick and sure as he sent the balls spinning off in every direction on the break, the six ball finding the corner pocket.

Picking up the chalk, he used it to coat the head of the cue stick while looking levelly at her. "So, now I'm abnormal. I could see how that might bother you. Gee, Syd, I'm surprised you allow me around the twins. I've got the even ones. Two ball in the center pocket." So saying, he bent to execute the shot.

The ball hit in the center of the pocket, and he stood up, walking around the table to assess his next shot.

"I'm not as rusty as I thought I might be. And it is good to be away from that typewriter. Anyway, getting back to you—I guess you must have majored in armchair psychology at one of the many schools you've attended—either that, or you need to find another project to occupy your mind now that Sydney's Folly is almost completed."

Sydney loved Blake. Really. She loved him. She knew she did, and had known it for weeks, even if she hadn't admitted it to herself until a couple of days ago. So why was she suddenly finding it so difficult not to take her cue stick and beat him repeatedly over the head with it?

"Don't be facetious, Blake," she warned, watching as he missed his next shot. "I'm trying to be serious here. Besides, I know not everybody stays in school until they're twenty-five. I've just always enjoyed school."

"Facetious? Me? Never," Blake countered, hopping onto one of the high-backed stools that lined one side of the room. "I think the five ball is your best bet, Dr. Blackmun, unless you were frightened by a five ball in your infancy, in which case, I'd try for the seven." His voice had taken on a hard edge.

"That's it, Blake," she answered encouragingly. "You're finally getting angry! Good! Get so angry, you tell me to mind my own business. That's what I've been waiting to hear since I got back from Paris."

Blake looked at her blankly. "That's it? You're kidding, aren't you?" he asked, confused. "You wanted me to yell at you? *That's* what has been bothering you?"

She nodded, smiling. "Yup. I stuck my nose in where it didn't belong—telling you that you had to come to terms with losing your basketball career—and you should have chopped it off. But you didn't. You just walked away. Even Pops said you had every right to wring my neck."

"I think I like your stepfather," Blake told her. "But he's right, Sydney, and I did resent being treated like some sort of reclamation project, and still do, even if you meant well. I can't say I didn't appreciate your help with my story, but I've been out on my own for a lot of years now, and really don't need your help in my personal life."

"Exactly! And it wasn't as if I hadn't done it before, either. Remember how I tried to get Wilbur to read your play? You didn't get as angry with me then as a lot of people might have. You didn't even tell me to shut up. You're beginning to do a pretty good job of it today, though, I have to admit. Yes, I feel much better now, and I'll bet you do too. And I will go for the five, thank you."

She sized up the shot quickly and sank it with ease. "Now, the seven into the corner, and I'll bank the eleven off it into the side pocket."

Both balls fell, leaving her with a fairly good shot at the nine ball. Out of the corners of her eyes she could see the muscles in Blake's neck begin to tighten. He had to be thinking about how she had pushed him, arguing with him about the way he had turned his back on his dream without ever really coming to terms with what had happened to him.

A smart person would call it a day, but she had to go on. She had to keep pushing, she had to know if she should begin to think about how she was going to get through the rest of her life without him. Because, she felt certain, if Blake couldn't come to terms with his lost dream, he'd never really dare to dream about the future.

The nine ball didn't fall, and Sydney retired to one of the stools. "So, Blake," she said lightly, "let's try it again, and see if you cut my nose off this time around. We're playing pool, but let's talk about another game—basketball. You remember basketball, don't you? Are you, like Sam, going to find another way to live your dreams?"

Blake picked up the cue ball and set it inside the rack that rested on the side table. "Game's over—both of them." He opened his mouth, as if to speak, then shook his head. "You know, Syd, you're really something else. That business about my not being angry with you was just a smoke screen, wasn't it? You had a whole other subject in mind all along, didn't you?

"But what *really* kills me," Blake said, replacing his cue, "what really makes this whole thing so ironic, is that you haven't the faintest idea of what to do with your own life. You've admitted it, out of your own mouth. You play all summer here at the beach, then play at school for the rest of the year—the professional student."

He walked over to face her, his expression hard and strained. "For crying out loud, Syd, what gives you the right to meddle with my head when you don't have yours on straight?"

She immediately bristled. "And what is that supposed to mean?"

"Do I have to spell it out for you? It means," Blake said, advancing on her so purposefully that she involuntarily backed up a step, "that you don't have the faintest idea of what you want to do with your *own* life. Sydney's Folly is just one of your summer toys. God, you've all but admitted trying to turn me into another one of your summer projects! Don't you think you ought to figure out what you want to do with your own life before you start meddling in anyone else's?"

She was too confused to be angry. "There you go again, talking about my projects. Yes, Sydney's Folly was a spur-of-the-moment decision, but I don't regret it. And I do so know what I'm going to do with my life," she added, stung. "I already told you, if you'd only listened—I start school in the fall. I can't wait to be with the kids."

"I've heard you, Sydney," Blake countered. "What's it going to be this year—some exclusive cooking school in Connecticut? According to the twins, you won't rest until you come up with the perfect meat loaf."

Sydney was beginning to feel dizzy. They were going around in verbal circles, first touching on Blake's inability to come to terms with the loss of his basketball career, and now centering on what he seemed to believe was her aimless, flighty life-style. Nowhere in this conversation were they talking about the most important thing of all—whether or not they were going to face the future together.

She ran her fingers through her hair, causing it to fall sleekly behind her ears. "Can we back up for a minute here, Blake? I don't know what you're talking about. I've told you I am starting school in the fall, yes. But I'll be *teaching*, not taking courses. I've accepted a position with the *school district* in Fairfield, Connecticut, teaching special education at the intermediate level. Didn't you understand that? Didn't I make myself clear?''

Blake collapsed against the wall, as if all of the strength had left his body. ''Teaching?'' he murmured, shaking his head. ''All this time I've been thinking—'' he looked at Sydney, his expression still faintly incredulous. ''How could I have misunderstood? How could I have been so wrong?''

Suddenly it all came together for Sydney. All Blake's teasing about her projects, her merit badges, her stones for remembrance. He had seen her as flighty, interested in living only for the moment—the sort of woman with whom he could have a lighthearted summer fling and then walk away, heart whole—because that way he wouldn't have to take a chance on losing another dream.

''Maybe because you didn't *want* to see anything but the flighty Sydney,'' she suggested when he didn't say anything else. ''And why should you? I'm just as guilty as you are. I saw only what I wanted to see as well. We're both guilty of looking for things that aren't there. Isn't that always the way of summer romances? Oh, damn it, Blake—get out of here!''

She heard him calling after her as she ran up the stairs, but she didn't stop, didn't turn back. She slammed the door to her room, locked it behind her, and fell onto the bed as sobs overtook her.

Pundit wasn't a bad dog, but he was a big dog and, it seemed, a lonely one, who tended to get into all sorts of trouble when his young masters weren't around to play with him. After putting the boys on the plane and ordering new draperies for the sun room—Pundit seemed to have tried climbing them—Sydney didn't have any other choice but to bring the Labrador back to Delancey Place with her.

The day after her argument with Blake she had considered moving into her parents' condo, which Wilbur and Clarissa had vacated in order to return to Manhattan in time for Clarissa to audition for a toothpaste commercial, with Clarissa in the supporting role of dancing dental floss.

But Sydney knew that leaving Delancey Place could only be considered the height of cowardice, even now, with the twins no longer there to keep her company. She had run away once, all the way to Paris, but she wasn't going to put her tail between her legs and make the same blunder twice. Besides, she didn't think she could survive being that far away from Blake.

Blake. She had seen him only in passing since her emotional eruption that day in the billiards room. He had been cordial, maddeningly friendly actually, when they met; almost as if they had only been chums, rather than near lovers. But that was all. Somehow, he always made sure that they were never alone together.

Not that she had gone out of her way to seek him out, first nursing her anger and hurt, and then through sheer obstinacy. She was through playing Mary Poppins, and she was through taking all the steps. If he wanted her, if he truly loved her, the next step would have to come from him.

Thankfully, all the exterior work that she could do on Sydney's Folly had already been done before their last argument, and she had launched herself into a near frenzy of work on the interior, keeping her too busy to find time to think up ways of "accidentally" placing herself in Blake's path.

This dedication to Sydney's Folly had done wonders for the house, but she realized now—with she and Pundit sitting in the sparklingly complete kitchen, staring at each other—that she really didn't have anything more to do.

Tomorrow, she promised herself silently. Tomorrow she'd contact that retired couple she'd met to finalize plans about their taking over management of the place. Tomorrow she would start taking positive steps toward her future and try to map out the long, empty years that stretched ahead of her.

"Damn him!" Sydney jumped up from her chair to begin pacing around the kitchen, Pundit's big brown eyes watching her warily, as if he might be in line for punishment for something he hadn't done.

"Who does he think he is?" she asked the dog, leaning down to address Pundit. "Huh? Just because he was right? Oh, sure—he was right, all right. I don't need a brick to fall on my head to tell me I was wrong. Mom and Pops took care of that for me—along with Plague and Pestilence! I poked my nose in where it didn't belong, and Blake chopped it off for me. Or maybe I chopped it off myself—I'm not really sure about that part of it yet. But, all that to one side—who does Blake Mansfield think he is to do this to me? Who does he think he is to think I'm flighty? *Flighty!* Do I really give the impression of being flighty?''

Pundit tilted his head to one side quizzically and Sydney laughed out loud. ''Oh, what am I asking you for, anyway? Anybody who mistakes Pops's new briefcase for a chew toy shouldn't even consider answering questions. Now, where was I? Oh, yes. I was hating Blake. Hating Blake is easier than hating myself.''

She turned toward the window, looking to see if Blake's kitchen light was on, then whirled back to confront Pundit. ''He holds me at a distance, while he kept right on being friendly with Plague and Pestilence. Did you know that? Oh, yes, he sure did. Playing basketball, jumping the waves, walking with them on the boardwalk, beating them at miniature golf. God, but I hate him!

''Maybe he thinks he's giving me time to cool off,'' she said consideringly, leaning against the countertop. ''I *was* pretty upset. After all, he hasn't gone, and his light stays on late every night, as if he's working. It has been on past midnight every night for the past month. He has to be working on the play again. What else could he be doing? Hey, Pundit, you look hungry. Want some meat loaf?'' She pushed herself away from the counter and crossed to the refrigerator, yanking open the door as she continued to ramble out loud.

''I don't know if he knows it, but Blake sure has found a great way to rattle my cage. Well, let me tell you, Pundit, old boy, tomorrow it's all going to change. I don't care what Mom said. Now that the boys are out of the line of fire, it's time to go on the offensive! Tomorrow, first thing, I'm going to march right over there and have this out with him once and for— What's this?''

A thick manila portfolio was lying on the top shelf of the refrigerator, right next to what was left of her twelfth valiant attempt at meat loaf—the one the twins had heralded as a major breakthrough. She lifted the bundle out, absently kicking the door closed on the dog's promised midnight snack as she walked over to the table—stepping over Pundit—and sat down.

There was a note paper-clipped to the portfolio, written in Paul's neat printing. '''Sis,''' she read out loud, '''Blake said for me to put this where you'd be sure to find it when you came home. I figured you had to eat sometime. Neat, huh? As they say in Paris, *bon appétit.*'''

Her hands trembling, she removed the contents, a two-inch thick stack of typing paper, to read the title page. *Stones For Remembrance,* a novel by Blake Mansfield.

"A *novel?*" She turned her head, looking out the window to see that a light had come on in Blake's kitchen. "Oh, you wonderful, wonderful man," she said, feeling tears threatening behind her eyes. "I knew I was right to love you!"

The beach was steeped in a dense fog, even though the sun had begun to rise above the horizon, so that Sydney lost sight of Pundit as he ran along the sand

ahead of her, furiously barking at a group of noisy sea
gulls.

She held the manila portfolio close against her chest
as she walked, cradling it as she would a precious
crystal vase. *Stones For Remembrance* was precious.
Not just because it was a wonderful manuscript, but
because it had proved to her, in approximately sixty
thousand beautifully crafted words, that Blake
Mansfield loved Sydney Blackmun.

The old Sam Everett had been banished into liter-
ary limbo, and she didn't care if she ever saw him
again. Gone, too, was the play format, and Sydney
knew that to be a good decision. Only a novel could
really tell the new Sam's story.

"Sam and Mellie's story," she corrected, smiling
through the happy tears that had begun to fall in
Chapter Four and hadn't really stopped as she had
turned over the last page, leaving the two characters to
live out their happily-ever-after ending. Not that the
book was dripping with sentimentality, because it
wasn't.

Sam and Mellie still had some problems to work
out; they still argued over some things, and probably
always would. That was the beauty of the thing—it
was so entirely real. But the reader would know, as
Sydney knew, that Sam and Mellie would always have
each other—and the hope and determination that was
so necessary in any truly loving relationship.

Sydney had thought she would knock on Blake's
door at daybreak, but when she finally finished the
manuscript, she knew that Blake had other plans for
her. She might not always be biddable, but she would

indulge him this time by living out the final scene in the book.

Sam and Mellie had come together on a lonely stretch of beach in Cape Cod. New Jersey wasn't Massachusetts, but a beach was a beach. And this was their beach, hers and Blake's.

The only thing he couldn't have counted on was the fog. She raised a hand to her eyes, as if the action would help her to pierce the mist, helping her locate Blake.

"Good morning, Sydney."

She whirled about so quickly she nearly dropped the manuscript. "Blake!"

"None other. Whose horse is that?"

Sydney frowned, turning her head to see Pundit running up the beach, his long pink tongue lolling from side to side as his mouth opened in a friendly doggy grin.

"This is Pundit," she answered as the dog sniffed at Blake's feet. The dog seemed to have accepted him, lying down and dropping his large head onto his sandy paws. "But don't worry, he's not mine. I found him, but he really belongs to the twins."

Blake bent down to pat Pundit's head. *He looks wonderful this morning,* she thought, fighting the impulse to throw herself into his arms. His hair was endearingly windblown, he looked a little nervous, nearly exhausted, and she loved him so much she thought her heart was going to burst.

But it was his scene, and she knew she'd have to let him play it out his way. However, if he didn't stop petting that stupid dog and kiss her soon she was going to kick him!

"You've read it?" he asked, standing up straight once more as he pushed on the nosepiece of his glasses and nodded his head toward the portfolio. "Where did Paul put it?"

"Next to the world's greatest meat loaf," she answered absently, looking down at the portfolio as if there were some secret message hidden there that would help her figure out what to say next. "But that's another story."

"So? Did you like it—the novel, not the meat loaf? I've already heard about your campaign to prove that there's nothing you can't conquer. I've been keeping the boys in pizza and fries until you finally got it right. Now, answer me. What did you think?"

She closed her eyes and shook her head. "You really take the cake, Mansfield, do you know that? You know darn well I like it. How couldn't I? Sam, hiding from his disappointment in Cape Cod, and Mellie, pushing him, kicking and screaming at times, back into life. Who knows, now that Sam is back in medicine he might just discover a cure for the common cold, or something."

"Or something," Blake said, gently taking the portfolio out of her arms. "But you're right. First Mellie had to give him hell, shake him back to life, and make him realize that a life had room for more than one version of a dream. He also had to do some heavy apologizing for some misconceptions he had made about her."

"I thought your—*his* apology was wonderful. Mellie's heart would have had to be made of solid granite not to forgive him." Sydney felt tears threatening again, and she wanted to hold him so badly that her empty arms were beginning to ache. She spoke only to fill the silence. "How did you come up with a name like Mellie? It's very different."

He grinned, and she longed to kiss the laugh creases that formed in his cheeks. "It's short for Melbourne. It was the only other Australian city I could think of at the time. Sydney—I have a confession to make."

She tilted her head and looked at him quizzically, rather like Pundit had done with her the night before. "A confession? Is it about basketball?"

"Basketball? You've *got* to be kidding." Dropping the portfolio on the dry sand at his feet, Blake pulled Sydney lightly into his arms. "But we will talk about that later. I think we both already know I want to be involved with the game again. Working with Pete and Paul and the other kids down at the playground decided that for me—not that your constant nagging didn't have something to do with it. No, I want to talk to you about something else."

Sydney got very still, so that Pundit, always easily bored, lost interest and took off down the beach after another sea gull. "I'm listening, Blake."

He slid one arm around her slim waist, using his other hand to gently push her head against his chest. "I don't want you looking at me with those huge emerald eyes right now, Syd, or else I'll never get this out. It's about us—you and me—and what seems to have happened to us this summer."

His fingers slowly twisted through her long hair, to lightly caress her nape, and she felt tears stinging at the back of her eyes as she thrilled at his touch. "I thought we were having a summer romance. You know—a few laughs, a few kisses, and then promises to write once summer was over, knowing we'd never see each other again."

He took a deep breath, and Sydney's heart ached for him. "I told myself that was what we both wanted, but I was only fooling myself. Somewhere along the line it stopped being a game, for both of us, I hope. So, I guess you've already figured out what I want to say, having read the ending of my book, but I have to tell you, anyway. I love you, Sydney Blackmun. I love you more than I loved basketball, more than I love writing, more than I love life itself. I love you—and I never want our summer to end."

Sydney tilted her head back so that she could smile up into his eyes. "Oh, Blake," she said, sniffling, "that was even more beautiful than Sam's speech to Mellie. I love you, too. I love you so much!"

Then her smile faded for a moment, and she said, "You put me through the worst month of my life, Blake Mansfield, do you know that? I thought you had decided that your feelings for me were a temporary aberration and that I was nothing more than a scatterbrained, interfering idiot, trying to ruin your life."

Blake's smile lit Sydney's world with the power of a thousand sunrises. "No, I thought you were a wonderful, headstrong idiot, trying to run my life. There's a difference—I think. But I knew you'd have to remind me of what a jerk I'd been about your projects before we could put all of our misunderstandings behind us. Now, can we get on with the kissing, or do you have something else to say?''

Sydney was at a loss for words, but only momentarily. "Blake!" she exclaimed, inspiration striking. Why hadn't she seen it before? It was so perfect! "Do you have any idea how wonderful all this is? I mean, you're a writer, and a writer can write anywhere. We can live in Fairfield during the school year, and come back to Sydney's Folly every summer. I told you I'm going to keep a room for myself. We can stay there at first, and then later, after the children come, we can—"

"Syd!"

She looked up at him, grinning sheepishly as she bit back the rest of her words. "Don't, darling. I'll say it for you: 'Syd—shut up!' "

"You got it, lady," Blake answered as his arms slid around her and his mouth came down to claim hers in a kiss that said more than any sixty thousand words, no matter how well written, ever could.

Neither of them noticed that the sun had burned away the fog, or that some other early morning visitors to the beach were standing nearby, softly applauding their happy ending.

Epilogue

"They're here, Blake!" Sydney called in the direction of the stairs, kicking the front door shut on the February chill that came in off the Long Island Sound. She had met the deliveryman as she had pulled into the driveway, and she had left him still counting the extremely generous tip she had pushed into his hand as she rushed toward the house. "Hurry up, or I'll open the box myself!"

Blake appeared at the head of the landing, pushing at the nosepiece of his glasses as he looked down into the foyer of the century-old renovated farmhouse. "My advance copies of *Stones for Remembrance?* For God's sake, Syd, put them down somewhere. Wilbur said he was sending thirty copies. They have to weigh a ton."

Sydney walked into the living room, obediently placed the large box in the center of the oriental rug

Blake had given her for Christmas, and shrugged out of her coat. "Get the letter opener from the desk, darling. This tape is stronger than the box. Hurry. I can't wait to see inside!"

Blake picked up the letter opener, retrieved her coat from the floor and placed it on a nearby chair, then dropped down beside his wife, crossing his long legs in front of him. "You've already seen the cover. Wilbur showed us the mock-up when we visited your parents at Christmas, remember?"

She watched impatiently as Blake slit open the box, and then reached inside, scattering packing pellets in every direction as she pulled out the top copy. Scarcely glancing at the cover, she opened the book carefully, turning pages until she got to the dedication.

"'There are many stones strewn in our paths from the cradle to the grave;'" she read out loud in a hushed voice, "'stones to stumble over, stones that block our way, and stones we use to build walls around ourselves, keeping away our dreams. But there are also very special stones, building pathways to our hearts, portals to our souls, and safe harbors for our dreams. To my wife, Sydney Blackmun Mansfield, who taught me the difference. I love you.'"

She closed the book, gently rubbing her hand over the cover as she blinked away sudden tears. "You never let me see the dedication. I've waited so long to read this, but it's been worth every moment of the wait. Blake—I feel so humble, and so very, very lucky."

Blake pulled her into his arms, one hand going to the soft swell of her belly, where his child grew inside her. "You don't have a corner on luck, Syd. I didn't think anybody could be as happy as we are, especially when you consider our 'rocky' start—pardon the pun. Now, come on," he said, pulling her to her feet, "it's time for your nap."

Her bottom lip came out in an exaggerated pout. "I don't want to sleep, Blake. You know we only had a half day at school today and I had the class watch a movie, *Mary Poppins*, so I've plenty of time to rest. Now I want to read your book. Cover to cover. Books always look different once they're in print."

He ignored her, guiding her toward the couch that faced the glowing fireplace. "You'll be sound asleep in five minutes. You always are. There," he said, covering her with an afghan she had crocheted from a kit last month—another project successfully concluded. He handed her the book. "And you'd better still be here when I get back from the gym."

"Yes, darling. I just love it when you're masterful. Be sure to say hello to the boys for me," she murmured, her eyelids already heavy for, although she had suffered none of the early morning sickness so common to pregnancy, she was finding it impossible to make it through her fifth month without daily naps.

"And Father O'Hara—don't forget to say hello to him, too," she added, mentioning the pastor of the local church where Blake, to his and Sydney's constant delight, coached the seventh- and eighth-grade basketball team. "Tell him he had a lovely sermon last Sunday. I think it was on sin."

"It usually is," Blake pointed out, shrugging into his coat. "It's still hard to believe there could be so much sin in Connecticut.'' He had been working hard on his second novel all day and, although he didn't like leaving Sydney, there was this new run-and-shoot play he'd diagrammed last night that he couldn't wait to show to the boys.

He looked across at his wife, noticing again how her stomach seemed to be growing almost daily, and dared to ask, "Syd, when you saw Dr. Horvath today after school—did he happen to say anything about the baby's size?"

Sydney looked at her husband, seeing the faintly panicked expression in his eyes. "Size?" she repeated, hugging her secret to herself. "No, not that I can remember. Why?"

He walked back over to the couch and looked down at her. "No reason. It's just that twins sometimes run in families." He shivered, shaking his head as he dropped a kiss on Sydney's forehead and turned for the door. "Nah, it couldn't be."

"Have a nice time at your practice, darling," she said, intent on hugging her secret to herself for at least a little while longer. After all, today was the official publishing date of his first book, and she wanted him to savor his triumph for a little while.

"And hurry home, please. We'll have to celebrate your book tonight—among other things," she added under her breath as he was closing the door, so that he couldn't hear her.

Or so she thought. He was back in the living room in an instant, on his knees beside the couch. "What other things, Syd?" he asked, his gaze intently searching her face for an answer.

She took his head in her hands and lightly kissed his forehead, then giggled, unable to hide her wonderful news for another moment. "Oh, all right. Let's just say, darling, that Dr. Horvath did mention something today—*two* little somethings, to be exact. On your way home maybe you'd better pick up one of those books on what to name our babies. After all, Plague and Pestilence are already taken."

Blake raised his hands to cover hers, then drew her fingertips against his lips. "Sydney Blackmun Mansfield," he said, swallowing hard, "did I ever tell you that I love you? That I love you more than anything on this earth?"

Her emerald eyes shining with tears of joy, Sydney snuggled more deeply into the couch cushions and smiled at her husband. "I know, darling, and I love you too. As I've told you so many times—love and hope and determination make for the best happy endings."

Blake leaned forward to place a tender kiss on her lips. "It's easy to see who the writer is in this family. Not happy endings for us, darling, never happy endings—happily ever *afters*."

* * * * *

This is the season of giving, and Silhouette proudly offers you its sixth annual Christmas collection.

SILHOUETTE
Christmas Stories
1991

Experience the joys of a holiday romance and treasure these heartwarming stories by four award-winning Silhouette authors:

Phyllis Halldorson—"A Memorable Noel"
Peggy Webb—"I Heard the Rabbits Singing"
Naomi Horton—"Dreaming of Angels"
Heather Graham Pozzessere—"The Christmas Bride"

Discover this yuletide celebration—sit back and enjoy Silhouette's Christmas gift of love.

WRITTEN IN THE STARS

WHEN A CAPRICORN MAN MEETS A GEMINI WOMAN...

Wealthy dairy farmer Adam Challow's no-nonsense approach to life wavered when he met the enticing Gemini beauty, Donna Calvert. The normally steadfast Capricorn didn't want to trust his feelings, but Donna was simply irresistible! Joan Smith's FOR RICHER, FOR POORER is coming this January from Silhouette Romance. After all, it's WRITTEN IN THE STARS!

Available in January at your favorite retail outlet, or order your copy now by sending your name, address, zip or postal code, along with a check or money order for $2.59 (please do not send cash), plus 75¢ postage and handling ($1.00 in Canada), payable to Silhouette Reader Service to:

In the U.S.

3010 Walden Ave.
P.O. Box 1396
Buffalo, NY 14269-1396

In Canada

P.O. Box 609
Fort Erie, Ontario
L2A 5X3

Please specify book title with your order.
Canadian residents add applicable federal and provincial taxes.

SR192

Silhouette Romance®

Silhouette Romance

LONG, TALL TEXANS

DONAVAN
Diana Palmer

Diana Palmer's bestselling LONG, TALL TEXANS series continues with DONAVAN....

From the moment elegant Fay York walked into the bar
on the wrong side of town, rugged Texan Donavan
Langley knew she was trouble. But the lovely young innocent awoke a tenderness in him that he'd never
known...and a desire to make her a proposal she couldn't
refuse....

Don't miss DONAVAN by Diana Palmer, the ninth book
in her LONG, TALL TEXANS series. Coming in January...only from Silhouette Romance.   LTT192